## About the Author

Encouraging youngsters to read stories about magic and mystery is what Ngaire thinks writing is all about. Stories about angels were passed through Ngaire's family becoming more entertaining each time they were told. Ngaire is a strong believer in crystal and angel healing and would love the thought of youngsters' imaginations running wild and asking for help from their angels whenever needed. Though angels are a relaxing thought, her real enjoyment is telling scary stories to her two children. Ngaire lives happily with her family in Hertfordshire where she grew up being told ghost stories and stories of magic and intrigue.

ANGELS GODS WITCHES

# N. M. Cockerill

---

ANGELS GODS WITCHES

Vanguard Press

A CIP catalogue record for this title is
available from the British Library.

ISBN      978 1 78465 800 7

*Vanguard Press is an imprint of
Pegasus Elliot MacKenzie Publishers Ltd.*
www.pegasuspublishers.com

First Published in 2020

**Vanguard Press
Sheraton House Castle Park
Cambridge England**

Printed & Bound in Great Britain

# Dedication

My world, Clarke and Giselle

# The Untold Tales of Louie the Young God and The Scroll of Light and Dark
## by N. M. Cockerill

## The Midnight Walk

It was a crystal-clear night in the land of Tarania. The moon was full and seemed larger and closer to the ground than usual.

The blanket of emerald-green grass that covered the meadow changed to a vibrant mix of magical colours, reflecting from the stars and midnight sky. Long grasses and wild flowers swayed and sparkled, soaking up the moon's powerful glow, as if recharging before daybreak.

The meadow's edge neighboured the scariest forest you will ever find, called the Border. It was guarded by the soldiers of Tarania who were ordered to stop anything going in and kill anything coming out.

Louie, a young god, had once again sneaked out of the palace for a walk to watch the stars and night creatures go about their nocturnal work. Life could be so boring in Tarania, nothing exciting ever happened until this particular midnight walk. Something strange caught Louie's eye. It was a flicker of candlelight moving towards the forest that stopped Louie still in his path.

Four cloaked figures crept suspiciously in amongst the trees vanishing into the thick blackness of the forest.

Although it was forbidden for anyone to enter, Louie often ignored this law.

He quickly followed the route the cloaked figures had taken and it wasn't long before the flicker of light was back in sight.

Louie needed to get off the ground to see what was happening without being caught by the cloaked figures or the soldiers, so he climbed an old knotted tree and tucked himself into the nook of a branch.

Louie watched and listened, trying his hardest to hear what the creatures were saying. They were definitely arguing but the words weren't clear.

The figures stopped and huddled together circling the light.

Louie climbed higher to see more and managed to stretch himself out onto a branch wrapping his arms and legs around it to stay on.

Cautiously letting go with one arm Louie fumbled around blindly in his satchel, eventually pulling out a small telescope. Awkwardly he put it up to his eye trying not to loosen his grip on the branch. It worked, he focused in on them and saw they were all looking at a map.

The figures huddled for what seemed like ages pointing at the piece of parchment and arguing. Louie's grip on the branch started slipping so he shuffled along to the far tip of the branch praying he didn't make a sound. He listened intently making out words here and there about a magic scroll and a witch. Suddenly without warning the parchment they'd been holding was screwed up into a ball and thrown on the ground. The half-pint creatures squealed with excitement in a high-pitched noise.

Sparks of light flew up from the soil followed by an electric green mist that seeped out from the ground covering the bottom of their cloaks. The soil beneath them evaporated leaving the four cloaked figures hovering effortlessly above what was now a large hole in the forest's floor.

The figures, one by one, lowered into the ground, the last looking over its shoulder to check they hadn't been seen. Within moments they'd all disappeared.

Louie, still hanging on for his life didn't move.

"Whoa, what just happened? Can't believe the soldiers missed this," he said to himself. Not wanting to be too hasty in case they came back up, he waited before climbing down from the tree and followed them.

The Border had always fascinated Louie. He would often sit in the meadow that ran alongside The Border hoping to catch a glimpse of the hideous creatures that lived in there. Usually the only thing that would spook him would be the ancient trees whispering to one another in their gruff husky old voices. Nothing had ever happened until now.

The forest had a tendency to stay dark during the day making it even less inviting than it already was. The vast eerie ground left you feeling unwanted and worthless. It was full of mystical dark spells and creepy inhabitants stopping uninvited visitors from passing through.

At night it had been known for soldiers patrolling the forest to just disappear. Legend says that angered ghosts would trick them into seeing shadows causing them to run into the heart of the forest, then when they were so far in they'd pounce like a pack of wolves stripping the soldier of his flesh and finish by swallowing his soul. Louie throve on these legends and loved telling the stories to his friends.

All that being said Tarania was actually a very peaceful world as was its neighbour Verlum. Tarania was the Land of the Gods and Verlum the Land of angels. The two worlds were separated by the thick spooky forest which was called 'the Border' by local folk. It was forbidden for anything or anyone to cross into the Border unless agreed by the keepers of either kingdom.

On the Taranian side of the forest the majority of land was filled with emerald-green valleys outlined with vivid coloured flowers and sparkling waterfalls that flowed from soft rocks embedded in the gentle hills. The water escaping the clear pools, at the bottom of the waterfalls, trickled into the rivers that ran through Tarania providing homes for the animals and fairy folk that throve on the river banks.

The villages within Tarania differed from one to the other depending on the type of 'being' that had settled there. They were scattered across the land but all had a view of the palace set high on the tallest of all peaks. This was Louie's home.

All the villages bustled during the day with markets, as the various folk went about their daily business, ranging from many professions like carpenters to fairy dust collectors, toadstool makers to unicorn wing menders.

The forest, on the other hand, was an intimidating thick buff of old tall trees that changed drastically the further into the forest they grew. It was not the place to go. Ever.

Louie had just celebrated his thirteenth birthday. He was a good-looking boy with golden waves of blond hair to his jaw, that he habitually tucked behind his ears, and piercing green eyes that struck you at first glance. He carried the strong square jaw passed down through the generation of male gods and a dimple in his left cheek that the girls found charming and cute when he smiled.

Louie was tall for his age and carried the athletic godly shape of square shoulders with accentuated muscles in his arms and chest with a small waist.

Being a young god, he was a born athlete and luckily enjoyed all sports like most youngsters his age in Tarania. Though not a straight-A student Louie made up for it with his common sense and loved school mainly because of the laugh he had with his friends.

Classmates at school didn't treat him as royalty, and he was certainly not the type to crave for the 'highness' treatment like some of his cousins did.

Though one day he would take his father's place on the throne, he tried to make the most of his freedom whilst he had it. He wouldn't start the serious training of a god until his sixteenth birthday.

Being the son of a god had its drawback. He was taught to set an example to others and had been known to feel the pressure of people watching his every move. A select few teachers at the school took pleasure in bullying him in front of his classmates to prove a point and were extra strict with him, making it unpleasant at times but Louie knew they weren't the greatest supporters of the gods.

Louie was very close to his father, Druce, who although quite strict, allowed his son to go about his childhood without the worries of the kingdom on his shoulders. He had many uncles, the closest was his father's youngest brother Aster. The other uncles were scattered around Tarania leaving Druce and Aster in charge of the ancient family palace. The other brothers were happy to live off the name of their godly heritage without having to deal with the worries of the land.

Aster was in charge of Tarania's army. The army's main duty was to patrol the forest between Verlum and Tarania, making sure no one entered from Verlum without permission and vice versa. They also made sure the laws of the land were adhered to. Aster took great pride in his army and this showed through the commitment his soldiers had to him and Tarania.

Though Tarania was a world for the gods, there were many other beings other than gods living within it. The beings were from a mixture of different creations, many of which had the blood of the gods in their veins but through the ages decided their paths were with creations other than the gods, therefore creating a land full of variety.

The main family of true-blood gods was Louie's family.

# The Tunnel Below

Louie slowly climbed down from the tree trying not to make a sound. His feet gently touched the forest floor, tiptoes first; he crouched down at the huge roots to consider his next move. He was about fifty metres from the hole in the ground and could see the ideal route to get to it. He'd have to be quick; the soldiers were never far away from any part of the forest and if he was caught, he would be in huge trouble.

Standing up and running was too risky so he decided to get down onto his tummy and crawl to where the hole had appeared. As he got closer his nose caught an awful stench of rotten eggs.

At that moment he heard footsteps crunching and froze. He lay face down on the prickly leaves and saw the feet of a soldier standing by his head. The soldier didn't move. Louie heard him take in a big sniff of air and let out a disapproving sound. He'd obviously smelt the rotten eggs too. Louie held his breath and thought, 'How have I not been picked up and thrown into a carriage yet?' Louie couldn't believe his luck when the soldier started to move away as if walking around the smell.

He waited until he was alone once again and took a small dagger from his belt and wiped the blade clean with his well-worn cloak. Sliding it over the edge of the hole he used the reflection of the blade as a mirror to check no one was there.

Nothing but darkness.

'Good,' he thought.

Gulping a huge deep breath of courage, Louie swung his legs over into the gaping ground and at speed lowered himself down feet first. He fell down a straight drop for a couple of metres landing on his bottom when he reached the main tunnel.

The smell of freshly dug soil immediately hit his nostrils followed by the dusty unsettled air floating around him. Grabbing his nose quickly, Louie sneezed twice causing his ears to pop with the force of not allowing the full extent of his sneezing to reach outside his head. It worked. No sound was made.

Once inside the neck of the tunnel it widened with twists and turns gradually descending down.

After a few minutes in, the descent took a sudden drop causing Louie to lose his footing and slip on something. He bent down and touched his foot; it felt thick, wet and slimy. Rummaging around in his cloak pocket, he pulled out a small jar with his helpful, rather podgy, glow-worm in for light and held it to his feet.

*Green slime?*

Pulling a face of disgust Louie wiped the slime from his hands onto his cloak not realising until it was too late just how potent the stench from the slime was. Now, on his cloak, it wafted up to his nose whenever his legs moved; he couldn't help but pull the same face of disgust every time the whiff hit him.

Popping the helpful little glow-worm back in his pocket, in case the light was seen from a distance, he carried on.

After combating the first steep decline, Louie heard falling rubble in the distance. He stopped abruptly. His heart pounded in his ears and chest. He felt a rush of panic shower over his body and realised he'd be trapped if anyone started to come back up the tunnel.

"What am I doing?" Louie whispered to himself shaking his head in a moment of sanity. "I should've thought this through properly."

Louie stayed still not moving a muscle, the sound of his heart still pounded loudly in his ears.

"No," he said to himself angrily, looking back up the way he'd come. "Keep going, it's just a bit of loose soil falling from the tunnel walls."

Louie carried on deeper and deeper into the tunnel and below the roots of the forest. He couldn't see his hands in front of his face; the air was the blackest of black. All his senses were electrically charged, the smell was intense, his vision was void and his ears were sharp.

Louie heard voices in the distance and though he couldn't see he closed his eyes anyway hoping it would improve his hearing. Unable to make out what was being said, he thought he heard a different language being spoken.

Knowing he was getting closer to whatever entered the tunnel he continued on for, what felt like, miles. The tunnel narrowed causing Louie's broad shoulders to brush the soil at the sides.

He saw a glow of light ahead. "This must be the end of the tunnel." Repeating the words again in his head Louie realised there was still no plan. "End of the tunnel! Now what?"

The ground flattened out and led to a sharp bend to Louie's left. With relief for a breather he waited a moment listening for anything that may be hiding around the corner, then slid his dagger out from under his belt and once again used it as a mirror. The light was dim. The dagger reflected what looked like a cave with no movement from within.

Very quietly Louie pulled himself around the bend and out of the tunnel. Louie now stood in a small unassuming cave lit by candlelight.

The walls were low and packed solid with brown and grey wet clay, making the air inside damp and musky smelling. The ceiling was dome shaped allowing Louie to stand up straight, though there wasn't very much room for manoeuvre. On the ground, in the centre of the cave, lay a whirlpool turquoise and white in colour. The water rushed dramatically around inside the pool making it hard for Louie to see into it. He bent down and knelt at the edge, to get a better view he leant over the water. The frantic waves splashed his face intermittently annoying Louie so much he slapped his hand down on the pool's face. He stood up now wetter and less patient, having gained nothing.

Louie found an area of his cloak, that hadn't been slimed, and dried his face and neck. It was then that Louie looked down towards the opposite side from where he was and noticed a pile of cloaks.

Louie's mind started to wander as he looked about the cave for anything else that might explain why someone, or something, would want to build this tunnel. As Louie bent down to interrogate the cloaks the bubbles in the whirlpool became even more erratic. Louie dropped his vision into the pool and saw a dark, half-sized shape approaching the surface. The figure wasn't clear but Louie was sure this was what he'd seen going into the tunnel. It looked very similar to a creature Louie had only seen in drawings called an awgul.

Louie felt the panic shake his body and without a second thought he dived back into the tunnel and, using all his speed and strength, he scrambled quickly back up the way he had come slipping every now and again on what he guessed was green, smelly slime.

The green slime confirmed his suspicion that the figures in cloaks were in fact creatures called awguls.

At last the top. Gulping in the fresh air, once his head was level with the ground, he grabbed the soil as if his life depended on it and clambered back out onto the forest floor. Pulling his legs out quickly, in anticipation of something grabbing them, Louie quickly pushed himself far enough away from the hole to the roots of a tree where he sat and caught his breath.

Panting for breath with his head between his knees he started to calm down. He finally lifted his exhausted body up from the ground. Brushing slime and soil from his cloak and knees, Louie took note of exactly where he was so he could show his father.

"I have to tell Father immediately," Louie said out loud with a hint of panic.

"I can help with that," replied a deep voice.

Louie spun round to see who had hold of his hood. He should've guessed. Before he had a chance to argue one of the Taranian soldiers dragged him out of the forest with force; his feet barely touched the ground.

"Damn," Louie said under his breath. "Father is going to kill me."

Even though the soldiers had known Louie from birth, they showed no mercy when it came to the protection of Tarania. Louie was thrown into the back of a horse-drawn carriage decorated with gold and silver leaves surrounding Louie's family crest of a heart with a lightning bolt.

The soldier shouted, in his deep voice, to the head of the carriage. "To the palace, we have a trespasser."

He looked down at Louie, who was less than half his size in height, and shook his head. "Your father is not going to be happy with you, my boy."

"But I promise this time I've found something," Louie begged, whilst pointing to where he'd entered the ground. "Look there on the ground."

The soldier turned to see what Louie was pointing at. "There's nothing there," the soldier replied.

Louie stood up ready to argue but stopped, the soldier was right, the hole had disappeared. There was now nothing but dirt. No hole in the forest ground could be seen.

# The Throne Room

Druce shouted from his throne with a deep thundering godly voice. "Do not answer me back. I have warned you. It's forbidden for a reason and you must abide by the rules of the kingdom as everyone else does.

"If you were to be sensed by any of the Verlum watchers I would not be able to stop them from attacking. A war would then start between two worlds that have been at peace for generations and allies and friends of this family."

The echoing vibrations of his voice shook the large, marble room. Louie had tried to speak, but his father was in a rage like he'd never seen before. Louie felt his own anger boiling inside. Why did they always treat him like a child? All he wanted was for his father to listen. After all, this time was different to the other times he'd been caught.

"Why won't you let me tell you why I was there? You haven't given me a chance to speak." The words poured out of Louie's mouth before he could stop them; he would be punished for speaking back to his father in such a manner. He'd never spoken out of turn to any of his peers, but this was different, he had to say something even if it was in a way he didn't expect. This time it was important.

His father's face started to turn purple with rage but, just as he was about to explode, he was stopped by the sound of the throne room doors crashing open and thundering against the walls on the way. Louie was cut off from speaking and the silence was abrupt. Louie bowed immediately as the man entered.

The man, twice the size of Louie, was a younger version of his father, his blond wavy hair sat on his large intimidating square shoulders and his, well-polished, silver body armour rattled as he walked. This was Druce's younger brother Aster.

Though Aster was intimidating to look at he had a heart of gold and had always been very close to Louie, though did not allow bad behaviour and would punish Louie by making him feel the disappointment and let down caused to himself and Druce. It would work too: Louie hated his uncle being mad with him.

"Uncle," Louie said instantly, bowing with respect.

Taking no notice of his nephew bowing, Aster ignored Louie's presence in the room and continued intently towards Druce.

"What in the name of this kingdom has gone on?" the voice bellowed.

The anger was intense and caused black thunder clouds to emerge above the domed glass roof of the throne room. This time his uncle was really mad with him.

Louie knew that everyone in the kingdom would see the thunderclouds and know something was going on. He felt embarrassed for a split second before once again reality hit and reminded him he was in deep, deep trouble.

Druce stood up from his throne and shook his head as he took hold of the golden staff propped against the wall next to him.

"Brother," Druce started with less purple in his complexion than moments earlier.

"Save your breath, Druce," Aster said abruptly. "This must be the final time your son is going to interfere. I have commanded the army of this land since our parents and continue to keep the peace with our neighbouring world as our grandfathers requested, but your son will not let this be. Does he think he can carry out the job of a general for this army better than me? It is embarrassing." Aster slammed his fist hard onto the marble table.

Aster continued to ignore the fact that Louie was in the same room and in doing so made Louie feel appalled with his actions.

Druce moved slowly towards his brother not knowing what he could say to defend his son. Aster was, after all, right. Louie had well and truly had his last chance. The frustration and anger Aster felt was felt by Druce too. What was he to do? This was his only son, who would eventually take his throne.

Louie stood up. "May I speak?" he asked nervously, wondering if he would even be heard over the thundering noise above them.

Druce let out a sigh of despair and nodded in the hope that soon a resolution to this problem would enter his mind and an extra minute would assist. Druce returned to his throne and slowly sat down in such a manner he looked as if he had aged by 200 years.

Louie began by apologising to both his father and uncle.

"But," he continued, "something happened tonight."

Louie looked at his uncle who turned and sat on his throne next to Druce.

For a moment Louie hesitated knowing that what he was about to say was not going to go down well. The moment of hesitation passed and Louie took a deep breath. He started to explain his adventure from the moment he saw the candlelight moving into the Border. Neither Druce or Aster showed any emotion or interest until Louie got to the part they were talking about.

"…they mentioned a magical scroll and a name of a witch that I can't remember but started with an X."

Louie noticed that now they were actually paying attention. Aster had slid forward to the edge of his seat as if trying to get closer to hear the outcome of his story.

Aster and Druce looked at each other sharply but said nothing.

Louie continued. "Then I followed them into the hole which led to a tunnel that took me deep below the ground."

Louie moved towards his uncle and father as he continued explaining about the tunnel and whirlpool, finishing with his suspicion of awguls being the cloaked figures.

Louie finished his tale and feared his father's wrath. Druce and Aster sat still and silent in their thrones. No movement from either.

"How did this happen?" asked Aster sharply turning to his brother.

"We have to act immediately," Druce said urgently. "Someone is trying to carry out the ritual of light and dark; there will be only one ending." Druce lowered his head. "Why did we not see this coming, brother? We have known for centuries that the ceremony was a possibility during the eclipse."

Druce was interrupted by Aster who was now up out of his throne and pacing back and forth along the throne room.

"How could I have been blind to this? I've noticed the border patrols becoming busier, but I thought this was just down to youngsters playing pranks on our soldiers. Not for one moment had the thought of us being tested enter my mind." Aster slowly stopped pacing and turned to look at his brother Druce. "They have been testing our strengths and weaknesses for a few months."

"Aster, you couldn't have known that this was the situation."

Druce now rose from his throne and walked over to his brother who was stood at the marble table. Druce continued. "The magic of Es'trixia has been dormant for thousands of years; our ancestors were the last to write about this magic." Druce let out a long sigh and turned to Loiue.

"You have done well, my son, to bring this to our attention and I am so very sorry I shouted at you without hearing your side of events; you didn't deserve that. Do you realise the danger you have put yourself in, Louie? You are lucky to have returned from the tunnel alive."

Louie sat on the edge of his small throne and watched his father and uncle in anticipation. "What is going on?" he asked.

Druce knew that his son was now involved and had to be told everything. After all, his son had managed to enter a magical tunnel without being detected.

"I will show you," Druce said.

# The Sisters

Sat on his throne at the head of the silver and gold marble table, Druce lifted his golden staff and effortlessly banged the bottom of it on the floor. A small quake was felt beneath their feet followed by a puff of white smoke that shot out the top, evaporating into hundreds of pictures around the room, some small, some life sized, some static and some moving.

The candlelit chandeliers that sat suspended above the long table flickered to a dim light, accentuating the already large shadows of Louie's father and uncle, and allowed one of the motionless pictures that hovered above the centre of the table to shine clearly.

Druce waved his hand at the picture and all three gods watched as it came to life in front of them.

The picture began to move slowly before reaching normal speed. It was set deep in a forest at night. Three beautiful young girls, older than Louie, sat around a large iron cauldron that balanced above the bright burning flames of a fire, each of its turned-up feet placed on logs for stability.

The girls were sisters but each differed in looks. The blonde-haired sister chanted a spell with her eyes closed and head towards the sky. The black-haired sister stirred the contents of the cauldron whilst the red-haired sister sprinkled herbs into it.

Silence within the forest was sudden and cutting.

The chanting stopped and the fire lowered to a halo glow of orange; the sisters knelt at the bulbous bottom of the cauldron as if praying.

Then suddenly a burst of red and green flames exploded out of the cauldron and shot high into the midnight sky.

The sisters raised their heads and watched the cauldron shake erratically as if threatening to tip. A few moments later a giant serpent shot out of the cauldron and appeared at the top of the dancing flames. Its red snake-like body swayed whilst it got its balance and using its dragon wings to help, it was finally stable. The creature slowly lifted its head exposing great horns and the unexpected face of a god.

"Father," the blonde sister shouted with happiness.

"My beautiful daughters," the creature said with heartfelt emotion. "Why do you summon me from the depths of the underworld?"

"Father," the black-haired sister started, "we need your help. We had no one else to turn to. Our worlds are at war and we can't stop it. The elders have pushed us away and we are now afraid that evil has finally over taken good. It is starting to control everything."

The blonde sister nodded with agreement. "The worlds are being destroyed every moment the gods and angels are at battle with each other."

The red-haired sister rose up off her knees in the hope to get closer to the beast hovering above the flames.

"We don't know how to solve this. We have dark blood from your father, a god, who now lives in the darkest pit of the universe and light blood from Mother who is the daughter of angels, but still, we are unable to stop this war with our powers of light and dark blood.

"The gods and angels are at battle to rule each other's worlds. Magic has become dark and strong. We can't defeat it to take control and restore the balance. A curse has spread across all lands sending the most reasonable leaders into disarray."

As the sisters stood looking up at their father an astounding ray of white light rushed down from the sky hitting the ground, causing sparks to bounce close to the cauldron.

A bright light emerged from the sparks on the ground and shimmered into a beautiful woman.

"Mother?" questioned the blonde sister. "Is that you?"

"Yes, my precious girl," said a soft angelic voice.

The black-haired sister stood up slowly and walked towards the glowing aura that was covering the female body of their mother. She threw her arms around her mother followed by her two sisters.

The serpent figure bowed in her presence. "Alauria, it has been many, many years." He raised his head and took in the beauty of his beautiful wife. "You are more beautiful than I remember. It has been hell's joy to keep us apart since our vows of love, though we are lucky to have three beautiful daughters that continue your beauty and the blood of light and dark. I miss you in my life, Alauria."

"And you in mine, Thelor," Alauria replied.

Alauria gazed at the beast in front of her, knowing this was her husband; she felt her heart sink for a moment. Seeing him again whether in beast form or not she saw into the soul that had once shone brightly through dark blood. She missed him so very much every moment they were apart, but had to keep strong for them both; this was not the time to reminisce.

"I don't have long on this soil so I will be quick in my explanation." She stroked the hair of her daughters one at a time and brushed the palms of her warm hands across their cheeks whilst she explained. "I felt it my duty to warn my three daughters of what I know. The battle, between the gods and angels has, now, become fierce and bloody. At the centre of this fight is a scroll that was given to your father and I upon our marriage. Friendships and alliances between dark and light were born between both worlds upon our marriage. This encouraged a balance and understanding that both bloodlines strove for the same things in life. It proved that love between dark and light blood was possible even though it was thought to be an impossible and disastrous to mix."

Alauria glided around her daughters. "Our marriage was celebrated throughout the angels and the gods. It meant the petty wars between the two worlds had a reason to end.

"The scroll was seen as a sacred binding signed by both of us with our blood upon our marriage and as proof to those who didn't believe. The kings of the gods and highest angels stood side by side and watched as our blood floated from our hands and entwined above the scroll. This was a sure sign that our different bloods could be as one. Never had the bloods met before."

"What did the leaders of the gods and angels think about this binding of your love?" asked the blonde sister.

"The gods and angels thought the love between your father and I was a sign from the universe proving that peace was something that grew with time and had nothing to do with creation by the elders: it was a sure sign for battles to stop."

"What happened to the scroll once were married?"

"The scroll was enchanted with a prayer from the angels and encapsulated in a magical golden case from the gods and kept at the table of elders to remind everyone that you can overcome the unthought-of with peace, love, time and trust but also for safekeeping too."

"So how did everything become so horrible?"

"The main advisor to the elders was an angel called Julique. He and I had been friends at school. His feelings for me were stronger than mine were for him. He was disgusted that your father and I got along and tried so hard to win my affection. One day I had to explain to him that I was in love with your father. Julique was distraught and disgusted at the thought of me not only being in love with someone else but, even worse, a god. He didn't trust the joining of light and dark bloodlines, believing the gods' blood would eventually try and overpower the blood of the angels therefore abolishing the angel bloodline altogether. It was from that point on Julique changed. Something inside of him turned. He tried desperately to advise the elders against our marriage but they ignored him."

"What did he do?"

"This was the first time an elder had ignored the suggestions of an advisor. It was very embarrassing for Julique. Once the scroll was seated at the table it would be a constant reminder that he had lost me to a god. He wanted the scroll destroyed and the binding of our love broken. Julique came up with a plan to separate us and committed the most heinous of crimes in order to do so. Murder. He slaughtered three elders in cold blood and framed your father. He assumed that your father being sent to the underworld as punishment would be enough to break my love for him and the binding spell of the scroll, allowing it to then be destroyed and its power taken for himself. He was unaware that the scroll was bound with a second spell.

"After a while Julique received a place at the elders' table and managed to poison their minds, resulting in many turning their backs on the philosophy of the scroll and becoming darkened to the ways of peace. They started to believe that the mix of our two bloods had caused an evil to surface in your father resulting in him committing murder."

"What happened to Julique? Did he get away with the murders?"

"At first, yes, but not all went to plan for Julique. He became greedy and slipped up. The elders discovered he was the murderer and he fled the table vowing he would one day find the scroll and steal its power before destroying it."

"Why is it only now, so many years on, the worlds are fighting against each other?"

"The darkness of greed and hate that had grown within Julique whilst at the table has stayed and spread overpowering the elders. Julique has managed to poison them. He has since become a user of dark magic conjured by a very powerful witch named Es'trixia."

"What was the second spell attached to the scroll?"

"The scroll could be destroyed and its power taken if firstly our love was no more and secondly if the scroll was then opened under an eclipse of the sun and moon. What Julique failed to realise was that if our love was separated against our will, the scroll had been enchanted to disappear from the elders' table and hide itself in a secret location and that is exactly what happened, although Julique and others didn't find this out until he tried to steal it one night and, upon opening its casket, saw the scroll had disappeared. This sent him into an uncontrollable rage."

"What is the power Julique wants from the scroll?"

"Eternal life and power over all the universe. The scroll, once encapsulated, was spellbound to last for all eternity. But if opened under an eclipse the scroll would transfer its almighty powers to the one who holds it and, if held by one with evil in their heart, the evil would spread at the same time. It was enchanted this way for safekeeping if we were to both die.

"Julique has to be stopped. If he finds the scroll the worlds we've striven to build will be diseased with evil."

"But what can we do?" asked the red-haired sister.

"You are the only hope. Only the bloodline from the original holders of the scroll have the ability to find the scroll and keep it safely hidden. You must find it and hide it once again."

Back in the throne room the moving picture above the marble table shimmered away and was replaced by a picture of the three sisters, a while after their meeting with both parents, flying at speed above the sea that, once, separated Verlum and Tarania. The sky was black with rage.

Thunder, lightning and tornados spoke on behalf of the gods and angels, shaking the trees, water and air. The atmosphere was thick and fierce.

The blonde sister flew in between her two sisters then stopped abruptly. "Sisters!" she shouted. "Do you two feel that this is the place to rest the scroll?" Her words were whispers taken away by the wind. The world was loud at the moment and little could be heard anywhere above the treacherous storms around them.

Both sisters shouting against the wind replied, "Yes…"

The black-haired sister started chanting a spell. "Roots of soil, fluid of sea, become one whole and encase the scroll."

With those words the two separate lands either side of the water slowly made their way together, crawling begrudgingly on top of the sea. The sea became wild, fighting against the invasion, but eventually knew defeat. Slowly lowering its defences, it started sinking underneath the soils that allowed the lands to entwine their roots to become one.

Seconds before the lands fused, the red-haired sister took out a bright golden light from underneath her dark green cape and with force, and speed, threw the golden case into the very last open crack in the soil. As the light hit the entwining earth there was a small explosion and then it was gone. The crack closed.

The lands, finally, settled together and there was calm. All three sisters floated above where there was once water.

The black-haired sister started another spell. "Protection is love," and the other sisters joined in with the spell, "protection is peace, protection is always with light and dark. Safe the worlds will be, whilst evil will never see the scroll of light and dark."

The earth seemed to take one last deep breath in, then settled into stillness. A thick forest of trees quickly grew over the join between the two lands.

The sisters hovered in a circle then threw their arms around one another knowing they had saved the worlds from evil and had been lucky to survive the devastating magic of Es'trixia and Julique, who they had managed to lose only moments before closing the two lands.

Julique wanted the sisters dead.

The sisters took one more glance at one another before flying off in separate directions, each knowing they would never be able to meet again.

# Now What?

The pictures sucked back into the top of the golden staff at the side of Druce. The room was once again silent and out of darkness.

"Wow," breathed Louie.

"The elders eventually restored order: gods and angels stopped their bloodshed. But, certain things had been said and done by gods and angels to each other and it became apparent that the worlds would be peaceful if they were not shared by both. The sisters were secretly hidden by the elders one in each of the three lands: Tarania, Verlum and, the furthest, Herbaya. This made the balance of their powers even. Their mother, Alauria, had joined the elders at the table and their father, Thelor, was in the hell of the universe. There was light and dark blood in every place possible."

"Did the elders ever find out the truth?"

"Yes. Thankfully they did. When the truth was found out Thelor was offered his freedom but the thought of living his life alone without seeing his daughters and with Alauria being untouchable at the table, he felt it would be no different than staying where he was in the underworld.

"Thelor decided, with the elders' consent, he would stay and try and restore the souls of those who had made mistakes and wanted forgiveness for their crimes. Also he would be able to see his love Alauria because elders could sneak into the underworld at any time without being detected by anything that lived there. The one request he did make was to have the ability to shift from his monster form to his human form whenever he wanted."

"What happened to the sisters?" asked Louie.

"Even though the sisters were in hiding from Julique and Es'trixia they still made it their duty to show kindness to those who were turned to the darker side by Julique's hate for light and dark. This didn't work for everyone; some beings continued to terrorise those that mixed with the believers."

Druce moved in his throne. "You see, what Julique had done was spread rage and evil amongst the supporters of light and dark. They forgot how it felt to love or be loved. Darkness and evil were the influences amongst the majority.

"It took untold time for each sister to restore what they believed was enough 'good' to balance each world for the elders. Unfortunately the damage had been done. angels and gods lived separately and darkness in some souls lived on through generations. They became known as Blackhearts."

"The sisters sacrificed everything for our worlds," Louie added.

"For their efforts the elders did repay each sister with whatever it was they desired. The red-haired sister, Amber, asked that Herbeya be blessed with plants and flowers of every species allowing her to continue with her potions for ailments needed by those suffering. The black-haired sister, Onyx, asked that she be allowed to hunt Es'trixia and when found study the magic that Es'trixia owned with a view to turn it into good powerful magic. The blonde-haired sister, Clarity, asked that she be allowed to carry on the dark and light bloodline. All three sisters were granted their desire and lived peacefully doing exactly what they had asked for."

"How about Julique? What happened to him?"

"Julique is still out there somewhere." Druce pointed his staff to the domed glass ceiling of the throne room. "I am certain that the tunnel you found in the border has something to do with him, especially if he is using Es'trixia's magic. We need to think, very quickly, of the best way to deal with this, Aster," Druce turned to his brother once again.

Aster rose from his throne and walked towards the balcony at the end of the room.

The doors to the balcony were open allowing the warm breeze of the outside air to circulate inside. The view from the doors overlooked Tarania as far as the eye could see.

Aster quietly looked out for a moment before placing his hands on his hips just below the body armour that covered his upper body and started thinking aloud.

"So we are dealing with an angel, banished from the elders' table, that's using a magic greater than any other magic known in our worlds and we don't know where he is." He gave a sigh and shook his head in thought.

"Father," Louie began, "did Onyx banish Es'trixia? Surely she would be the perfect person to quiz about the magic we face. Is there anyone in her world that will know either where she is or her findings?"

Both Druce and Aster looked at each other.

"Son, we have less than one phase of the moon before the eclipse takes place. Aster and his army have to prepare themselves for what could be the last battle we ever fight as our world.

"We have to gather as much knowledge about the tunnels without anyone knowing and we have to be extra cautious of those around us; Julique will have Blackheart spies everywhere. You must be very wary of who you speak to and don't let anyone know of what we have found out unless you can trust them with your life. A surprise attack may be the only chance we have of defeating Julique. If we ever find him."

Louie replied still with questions. "The scroll of light and dark was hidden?"

"Yes," replied Druce.

"The worlds managed to repair the damage that Julique had caused between angels and gods?"

"In some cases this is true."

"So why is it now that Julique seems to think the scroll will tear the worlds apart again? We all live in separate lands now, surely no one will care for Julique?"

"Julique is and always has been power hungry; he is full of hate and revenge towards those in power. He wants to rule all the lands himself and has waited a very very long time to do so. The eclipse, that we are expecting, comes around every few thousand years and he may not get another chance.

"You see the elders are thought to be close to the end of their creation and it may be complete before the next eclipse in a hundred or so years. The scroll will be hidden forever when the elders have finished creating and eventually make one world."

"That's good, isn't it? If no one knows where it is surely no one can take it and destroy it?"

"The scroll has been masked yes, but it's whereabouts is easier to trace during the lead up to an eclipse. This is due to the veil between our worlds and the stars being thinner."

"Brother," Aster said, turning away from the open doors of the balcony towards both Druce and Louie. "I think we have to make the angels of Verlum aware of what we are faced with. We can't ignore the fact that Julique is one of them by blood. Maybe our armies can join forces and be ready to fight as one."

"Yes. It is a must and should be done right away."

"Father, I want to help. I can go to Verlum if allowed and see what I can find out about the magic of Es'trixia. Onyx settled there all them years ago and must have found out something about her magic."

"I'm not sure about this request. You have no fighting experience and I don't know how I feel about you entering into another world that is unknown by you and us."

Aster interrupted with a stern but patient voice. "Druce, we have very little time. We need to know what the magic's weak points are if any at all. Maybe it can be found. I will speak to the angels of Verlum immediately and ask for their permission in entering Louie into their world." Aster headed towards the throne room doors. "I will explain all that we know and be back here as soon as I can to update you. Louie, pack some items in a bag; you may be in their world for a while, if allowed. I will collect you in front of the palace gates and you will accompany me to Verlum." Aster stopped and hesitated for a moment.

Aster knew that he was asking a lot of his nephew; he had never properly trained to be in battle, and really, what did he know about quests to other lands? Aster knew that Louie's quest was probably the most important of all. If the magic had a weak point they had to know about it. This may be the only way to stop Julique from finding and destroying the scroll and gaining its power and someone young would be ignored by anyone else searching.

"Louie. Who would you trust with your life?"

Louie was taken aback by the question but took no more than a split second to answer. "Juggle and Petra. Why?"

"You are to take them with you on the quest. Go to them immediately. Tell them I have sent you and they are to help you with a project I have asked you to complete. They are to know nothing more until I say."

Louie nodded, taking in everything his uncle was saying.

"Tell their parents it is an emergency and I will speak to them as soon as I can, but if concerned to visit the palace. I still expect to see you back in front of the palace gates immediately." Aster left the throne room with purpose in his steps.

Druce looked at his son knowing this was a lot to ask of him. He would be the only one that could do this task undetected. Druce banged his staff on the floor creating, once again, a quake beneath their feet. Above the marble table hovered a wooden staff, smaller than his own. It floated down in front of Louie.

"This is yours, Louie. It is the last one left of its kind and has been handed down through generations. Take great care of it and don't let it out of your sight."

The staff shone with a light blue halo as it lowered and touched his hands. The wood was the smoothest Louie had ever felt with a misshaped handle at the top. It looked used, with notches indented up and down the stick part, but still felt solid and new.

"Thank you," Louie said slowly in awe of his new gift. He threw his arms around his father

"Goodbye," Druce said. 'I will anxiously await news. I love you, son."

"I love you too," Louie replied.

Louie turned and ran out of the throne room.

"Don't worry," Louie shouted back as he ran. "I will be fine."

# Friends for Life

Juggle and Petra were Louie's closest friends. On the first day of school the three where grouped together by the teacher and from then on it was impossible to separate them.

Juggle was a creation called a ferian: his mother was from the fairy clan and his father was an angel. He was a lot taller than Louie, but most beings from angel bloodlines were tall. He had olive skin and striking light-green, short spiky hair. His body was slender with long arms and legs and a set of large wings on his back, but unlike like angel wings that are feathered, his were layered with a very thin, chiffon-type see-through skin and very small feathers bordering the edge of each wing. Juggle had the kindness and sharp mind of an angel and the humour and mischievousness of a fairy. His name was given to him as a nickname that stuck at school as a young child through his larking around and incapability to juggle because of his clumsiness. He was a trustworthy friend to Louie.

Petra, who was known as 'P' to both Juggle and Louie, was from a family of healing witches. To most it would seem quite a straightforward creation but it isn't. Healing witches are able to transform into an animal they share their soul with. It was Petra's fate that the animal the elders chose for her was actually a bird. A large black raven. Its main purpose to protect.

Petra adored wildlife and took great interest in all species of birds. The other members of her family were paired to animals such as wolves, horses, bears and deer. Petra was the first ever to be paired with a bird. Her father would joke when she was young saying that the elders had run out of animals so had to start on the birds, and should count herself lucky not to be paired with something smaller, like a snail.

Petra was always full of life. It was hard to find anything she was afraid of. She was a pretty girl with long, shiny-black hair and streaks of purple and raven blue in it. When the sun caught her hair the black sparkled like fairy dust with subtle streaks of purple and blue fighting their way to the surface. Petra was a petite slim girl trained in most arts of fighting, but her overall skill was healing others with any natural source from the earth.

After quickly packing a bag of essentials, Louie ran to FenAir Cottage. Juggle's family worked locally so they were out when he got there.

Louie crashed, at speed through the front door to the cottage and ran straight upstairs to Juggle's room where he knew he would be studying.

"Juggle... Juggle," Louie panted.

"Hey, Louie," Juggle said calmly, not fazed by the panic Louie had expressed on entering his home.

"Juggle... you... have... to... come... now." Louie still couldn't manage a whole sentence without taking a breath in between each word. Continuing to pant for breath he stood staring at Juggle waiting for a reaction of panic too. The reaction didn't come, Juggle very rarely became panicked.

"Hey, Louie, calm down, you look worn out. Have you just run here from the palace?"

"Yes."

Louie sat on the edge of Juggle's bed putting his head between his knees hoping it would help him catch his breath.

"Do you want some water, Louie? I can..."

Louie cut him off mid-sentence. He could now breathe enough to push his sentence out. "Juggle. Listen to me. You have to come with me now. I cannot say any more while we are here. My uncle asked you to pack some essentials and we are to meet him at the palace gates immediately."

Juggle stood up quickly, knocking his chair over as a result. He realised this request must be important if the leader of the army was involved.

Louie continued, "While you pack I'm going to get P. We will pass on our way back and collect you. We have to get to the palace gates as soon as we can."

Juggle nodded listening to everything Louie said. "OK. I'll see you outside."

Louie ran back down the rickety staircase and out of the cottage. He now had to get to Petra's.

Petra lived in the woods not far from Juggle. Her parents built tree houses for each family member so they could have their own space to transform when necessary. Even though they were on their own in the tree house, it was only a few branches away until the next tree house and you could practically jump from one to the other.

Louie followed the grey, cobbled, stone path through the woods until he reached Petra's tree. Petra was standing at the bottom of her tree with a bag in her hand.

"Wondered when you'd turn up. You took ages."

Louie smiled as he remembered one of her many gifts. Panithapy. It was a form of mind-reading. If a family member or close friend was panicked or in trouble, Petra had the ability to receive the same thoughts from that person so she could help. It was the protection part of sharing her soul with a raven.

"How long have you known P?" Louie asked taking her bag from her hands.

"Since Aster asked you to collect Jug and me."

Petra and Louie started running away from the woods and back towards Juggle's cottage. They could see Juggle in the distance stretching his wings and running on the spot. Petra laughed at the sight; he was by no means a particularly sporty farian.

"Hey, guys. Shall I try and get us to the palace by air? Even if my wings get us halfway we will still save some time."

Louie and Petra stood beside Juggle and he grabbed hold of their waists. Their feet lifted off the ground and in no time at all they were gliding over the stream that ran from one side of the village, only just missing the rooftops of some of the thatched cottages along the way to the palace.

Juggle's wings were too delicate for long distance flying. It was the downfall of being his size with the wings of a fairy instead of an angel.

Juggle started to lose height not far from the palace. He glided back down and lowered both friends onto the sandy path. Once back on the ground they ran as fast as they could towards the golden gates of the palace in the near distance. The gates drifted open automatically and, in the courtyard, they could see Aster getting into the front of the royal horse-drawn carriage.

"Get on as quick as you can, please!" Aster shouted to them when they came into his sight. "No time to waste."

The three of them clambered up into the back of the carriage throwing their bags into the footwell at the front.

The sparkling white horses started moving immediately, throwing Juggle off balance who hadn't quite sat down properly yet. The horses powerfully rushed out of the gates and gathered more and more speed as the journey got underway.

Louie looked at his two best friends, sitting next to him, and wondered if he was getting them into something that was too dangerous and would live to regret they were ever involved. Petra placed her hand on his shoulder and shook her head.

"Don't think those thoughts, Louie. Dangerous or not we wouldn't want you to do this alone."

Louie smiled lightly and looked at the road ahead. The day had become night quicker than Louie had realised. They would arrive in Verlum by the height of the moon. He wondered what to expect in this whole other world he'd only dreamed of visiting.

Louie climbed into the front of the carriage and sat next to his uncle.

"Are you OK, Louie?" Aster asked.

"Yes, but I still have questions."

"Ask away."

"Where did Julique go?"

"No one knows. When the elders found out what he'd done he had already disappeared."

"Why hasn't he tried to look for the scroll himself?"

"The elders put a tracking spell on the three worlds so if Julique was to step into one of them again they would instantly know where to find him and he would then pay for his crime. He is what they call a fallen angel, an angel who has chosen evil over good."

Louie thought for a while, digesting everything his uncle said, then, continued with more questions.

"Why do we have to ask for permission to enter Verlum if we are trying to help?"

"When the war between angels and gods finally ended and the Border created, it was thought to be easier for the safety of each world if they had no contact between them. This gave everyone a chance to forget about the bad feeling that had destroyed the relationship between both. If anyone wanted to enter one or the other, they would have to explain why first, not giving anyone the opportunity to fuel another war. We have been at peace for a long time, Louie, but since it was always possible the scroll was buried in the Border, it was agreed the area should be protected in case evil began to look for it again."

Louie gazed at his uncle as he spoke, wondering what it would be like to have such power and strength.

"Louie," Aster started, "you are not to feel pressured into doing anything. If you are given permission to enter Verlum you may be swept away with the quest faster than you expect. I suggest you re-join your friends behind and think seriously about what we are asking of you."

"I have and I'll do everything I can to help."

Louie re-joined Juggle and Petra in the back of the carriage and closed his eyes imagining what

Verlum would look like when they got there. Within no time at all the three friends had fallen asleep, with help from the motion of the carriage.

# The Elders

The three worlds that existed in these times were small. They were each individually made by a selection of angels and gods, known as 'elders of the table'. It had, so far, taken thousands upon thousands of years to create the three worlds as they stood now: Herbeya, Tarania and Velrum.

At the start the angels and gods were given three worlds to create, the intention being, at the end of their creation, the three worlds would make one. The worlds would be grown by the angels and gods until it was thought they couldn't add any more to improve the existence of beings within the worlds.

The elders were a committee of six, three gods and three angels. They were the extreme royalty of the three worlds and when they were to die they would be replaced with individuals from their bloodline. Creation of every type of being, animal, plant, insect and material was discussed and agreed by the elders. The elders would have one individual with them at the table that would act as an adviser. The adviser would have been chosen for the job through the loyalty they had shown to the gods and angels.

Sitting in the sky above the three worlds, the elders' table stretched for miles. It could be seen as a streak of white light with a thin halo of rainbow colours swirled around it. Whether it was day or night the white light and rainbow colours shone bright in the sky, visible at all times.

Spread along the length of the table were maps and drawings of many different creations and lands. In the centre of the table on a clear crystal stand sat a giant gold-bound book. This contained thousands of pages referencing everything created. Each page showed a name, drawing and explanation of the creation.

This book was called *The Elders' Amazing Research and Teachings of Humanity* or *EARTH* for short, and never left the elders' table.

Each elder would have a team of creatures called scruffins working for them. In order to create something, many ingredients would have to be found and blended together. The scruffins would collect the ingredients from land and assist the elder in mixing and creating the creation. Scruffins were the cutest of all things created. They had short, pure-white bodies covered in the softest of fur; their little wings were a pale gold and twinkled when they flew about the table. With large round blue eyes, velvet ears that dangled by their cheeks and a round fluffy tail that wiggled when they walked. On collecting ingredients from the three worlds scruffins would be seen in the sky as balls of light hitting the ground, sometimes mistaken for shooting stars. If anyone on land was lucky enough to see a scruffin they would be granted a wish, but the wish would only be granted if it was a non-selfish wish, a wish that helped others.

The elders when selected for the table would be covered in an aura of protection, allowing them to continue with their work even if creations didn't go according to plan. If a creation ended up being either harmful or evil to others in the world the elders were forbidden to interfere. Nothing was ever made for a harmful or evil purpose, but the only thing that could never be controlled was free will and greed.

It was decided very early on by the elders that the creations would have to teach themselves, and one other, the morals of being good and not evil. The elders, initially, sent a teacher to each world to begin the cycle of goodness and still thousands of years on the cycle continues, but, there has been the odd creation that had fallen through the teaching cracks of morals and goodness.

The first 'being' was a creature named Cre'ment. He became the very first creation to be banished to a place underneath all three worlds. The evil he carried out was the murder of a poor little scruffin. This particular crime happened whilst the scruffin was collecting ingredients on land. Cre'ment saw the little fella land not far from his cave and decided that he wanted the creature for himself, so he captured him thinking he could provide him with unlimited wishes of power.

The scruffin couldn't do this, firstly he had been taken against his will and secondly because a wish cannot be for one's own gain.

When the scruffin failed to assist Cre'ment, he locked him in a cave starving and torturing him until one day the scruffin died from his sad heart. The elders wanted Cre'ment to suffer the same feelings as the poor little scruffin suffered, so they banished him to underneath the three worlds. The underworld.

The underworld is an evil, ugly world full of fire and ice, deadly serpents hunt anything with evil blood pumping through their veins. The pain of never being able to rest because you are being hunted, always feeling burnt or frozen, being constantly reminded of the pain you caused another and then being given the same pain through bolts of lightning sent to pierce your body.

Cre'ment begged for forgiveness and continues to beg every day he is there.

The elders being the creators of good, felt the underworld should be a place where all evil souls are sent. Cre'ment, having suffered the worst for the longest time, was the best to teach others to suffer for their evils.

The elders struck a deal with Cre'ment and it was decided that he would be the caretaker of the underworld and, for every evil soul banished, it was his job to put upon them the same feelings of fear he felt, until they were sorry for their actions. Once a 'true' sorry was heard by the elders, Cre'ment would have a moment's peace from the pain. In order for the souls to be sorry they would feel the pain Cre'ment had felt.

Cre'ment was and still is spreading the feeling of fear in the underworld and will continue to do so unless evil stops throughout the worlds. The only downside to this, is, the more evil that joins him the more power he has amongst the souls around him.

# Evil

Deep in the furthest pocket of the underworld an angel called Julique sat on his throne in a cave. Julique was untraceable in the underworld because he was an angel by blood. The elders spellbound the world making it possible for them to enter and leave the world without trace, originally to keep an eye on Cre'mant.

Julique didn't look so much like an angel any more. Yes his physique was tall and slender like an angel and he still had huge feathered wings, but the wings weren't pure white any more, they were a murky white with flecks of dark grey. His clothing was dark and dirty and his hair short and white with a streak of black at the front. His face was far from angelic. It had morphed into an evil face looking harsh and soulless. His chin was sharp and his eyes were far from the normal angelic silver, his pupils were black. His usual angelic porcelain skin had a rough worn look, his cheeks looked sunken and his cheekbones had become accentuated and the main feature of his face upon first glance. He looked unrecognisable as an angel.

Surrounded by black ice rocks and pools of molten fire he rose from his throne in a rage and now stood throwing fireballs from the palm of his hands at the small creatures in front of him: awguls.

"What do you mean there's no trace of the scroll!' he screamed. The sound of his voice and the explosion from his hands echoed within the cave bouncing off the rocks surrounding him.

"Sire," the lead awgul started with fear in his snorting hog voice. The awgul crept forward quivering with fear. "We dugged deep. Tunnel turnd t'water. We've bin in water. Saw noffin. Magic not broke spell, sire." The awgul shuffled back in line with the others, wiping green slime from his long snout of a nose and cowered wincing as he anticipated another fireball.

Julique's face turned purple with rage. "We're running out of time you disgusting little creatures and you are failing me. I will kill you if you don't find another way of getting to the scroll." Julique turned to the side of him and bellowed loudly to another creature. "Belf. Get me the witch. Tell her it's urgent and I need her NOW." Belf, a dwarf troll, bowed and scurried away through an arch and out the cave.

"I'll get you more magic and you'll continue doing as you're told." Slicking back his hair he composed himself as if the outburst was out of the ordinary. Julique walked over to a tall granite table in the corner of the cave and poured himself a drink from a black crystal decanter, filling it with some ice broken off the cave wall. Taking a slow sip of his snake venom cognac he turned back to the awguls.

"When the witch arrives you will listen to what she has to say and then leave this world to carry on the task you've been set. You are to kill anyone that stands in your way," he demanded, "and when you do eventually find the scroll you will send me a message through the star system." Julique reached behind his back and pulled out a short spear of mirrored glass from under his wing. He threw the spear to the leading awgul who caught it with both hands.

"Hold this up in the direction of the elders' table. When I see the light I'll be with you and the scroll instantly. Make sure you do it properly. The elders will want to know who has sent a star message and will be straight to where you are to investigate." The leading awgul slid the spear into the inside of his cloak nodding at Julique.

An electric green aura of light filled the archway that led into the cave. As the light approached, the green became more intense. The room was hit by the presence of Es'trixia, the witch.

Es'trixia's presence hit the cave and in her shrieking spiteful voice screamed at Julique, "What do you want? How dare you summon me like you do your minions." Es'trixia stood still in the archway with an angry electric charge of green light buzzing around her.

"Don't be like that, my queen." Julique, still with a glass in his hand, glided over to her. He placed one arm around her waist and gave her the glass he'd poured for himself. Es'trixia took the glass and sipped the iced liquid.

Relaxing, the electric aura dulled to a humming glow as she calmed.

"We have problems."

Julique relayed what the awgul had told him whilst he poured another drink for himself.

"Yes, that is a problem," Es'trixia replied in a calmer voice. "I can adapt the spell, but, if the scroll was there it should have worked. I'll find another way of getting the awguls across the boundaries in Verlum. It's not going to be easy. Onyx must have cast an extra spell within the soil. We need that spell to save time."

Es'trixia sat on Julique's throne, knowing he hated it when she did so, and casually sipped from her glass before continuing, "I'll have to conjure another spell to get the ugly little creatures into Verlum undetected. They shall go to her cottage." She looked at the awguls with disgust.

"If they," she said, pointing her drinking glass at the group of short brown hairy creatures in front of her, "can follow my spell correctly we can get away undetected. If they don't they will set the Border sensors off. This also means that when the cretins get close to the scroll there may be other sensor traps in place. I can only guess what these may be and plan accordingly."

Julique answered with reassurance. "I gave up my life to get my hands on that scroll. I like this plan, Es'trixia, you enhance the magic whilst the awguls look for the spell protecting it. Awguls," Julique abruptly turned to face them, "we need you to be prepared for this. You have to get what we need. Do not fail me. Now go and prepare."

The awguls bowed and disappeared from cave. Julique moved to where Es'trixia was relaxing in his throne.

"You are my wicked Queen Es'trixia. What would I do without you?"

"You would be rotting in this hell for eternity if I hadn't found you, that's what you'd be doing. You owe me your life, Julique, and I will hold you to that forever."

Throwing the crystal glass into a pool of fire, Es'trixia got off the throne and walked back to the arch and out of the cave. She was gone. Julique, knowing she was right, slumped back into his throne. He hated her arrogance, actually he despised everything about her. When this was over he'd find a way to kill her. The stupid witch wouldn't speak to him like that once he had the scroll in his hands. No one would. He'd control everything and be feared by all.

# Verlum

The carriage came to a halt at the edge of a cliff. Louie woke startled, forgetting where he was. Petra and Juggle had woken up a mile ago and laughed at Louie's reaction.

"Where are we?" asked Louie.

"We have reached the entrance to Verlum," replied Aster. Louie stood up from his seat.

"But we're on the edge of a cliff with nothing between here and the cliff in the distance."

Aster jumped down from the carriage hitting the ground with a solid thud. He walked over to the edge of the cliff and stopped. Standing still for a moment he looked up at the stars and moved a few steps to the side. Aster looked back down at the ground and after a short search picked up a branch that was resting against a rock. Aster continued with this odd behaviour by placing the branch upright into the centre of the rock. Louie looked at his friends and shrugged his shoulders.

The rock began to glow, then out the top of the branch shot a beam of light into the sky hitting a star directly above. The light spread over the emptiness between the two cliff faces making a bridge that stretched from one side to the other.

"Wow," Louie said in amazement. The three friends stood in the carriage and watched the transformation in front of their eyes. The bridge of light met with the cliff's edge on the opposite side forming an archway at the end. The light from the branch then disappeared leaving the bridge to glow on its own. An outline of an angel glided across the bridge towards Aster. Aster bowed his head as the angel finally stood in front of him.

"Aster my old friend, it's been a long time." The angel and Aster threw their arms around each other like long lost friends.

"Mardy, how long has it been? Too long?"

"Yes. Much too long," he replied.

Mardy was the same age as Aster. When he spoke there was a slight tune to his voice. Louie hadn't heard an accent like this before; it was a soft relaxing voice. He stood as tall as Aster, with a very similar physique too. This surprised Louie, he'd imagined all angels to be very slim and less athletic. Mardy had olive skin like Juggle's and piercing ice blue eyes outlined with a silver streak around the pupil. He was very well groomed; his platinum-coloured hair was short and neatly spiked on top, there was no rough or ready look to him like there was to Aster. He wore loose white trousers with a skintight vest accentuating his upper body muscles. The other angels followed suit and wore the same which made Louie wonder if this was a uniform. It was certainly a more relaxed uniform than that of the Taranian army.

Mardy's wings were the main feature. They were astounding to look at. The angel feathers that covered the wings hummed a very light gold glow. The full span of the wings upon extension was intimidating and powerful when they moved.

Aster and Mardy had grown up together, they were practically family. Their parents were good friends and had once lived in the same world together. When the angels moved to Verlum, Mardy's parents stayed in regular contact with Louie's grandparents. During the young part of Mardy's life his parents were both called to the elder's table and during the transition it was decided he would live at the palace in Tarania and learn the ways of the gods.

Mardy was royalty in Verlum and at that time he was too young to assist in decisions but not too young to learn about others in different worlds.

"Mardy, this is my nephew, Louie, and his two friends Petra and Juggle." With that all three jumped out of the carriage and stood next to Aster.

"Very pleased to meet you all." Mardy bowed graciously and turned back to Aster. "Shall we proceed into Verlum? I will settle you all in and Aster, you can explain exactly what is going on. The bridge guards will look after your horses while you're in

Verlum; they will be very well looked after until you wish to return."

Louie, Petra and Juggle grabbed their bags from the footwell of the carriage, whilst Aster reassured the horses of his return.

Mardy stepped back onto the bridge. "The bridge is safe for you to walk on; you may feel a warm sensation on your feet as you walk. This is quite normal for non-angel folk." Mardy smiled and continued to catch up on the years he and Aster had missed with each other.

"This is amazing," Petra said as she touched the handrail of the bridge. "It really does feel warm, almost comforting."

"The angels are known for spreading love. My dad says that angels provide love in everything they make, hence the feeling of warmth on the bridge," Juggle said, pleased he knew something Petra didn't.

The bridge crossed a drop that was at least a few hundred metres deep.

All five stepped off at the other end of the bridge and followed Mardy through the archway of pink light. As they walked through, each one of them was showered in a white rain of light. Mardy explained that this was a detector of evil and was used on all that passed into their world. After being showered the group followed a pathway through some bramble bushes, up a slight slope, and into a field full of blood-red flowers. On walking into the field the flowers moved out of the way of the visitors, as if saving themselves from being trampled on. The smell was unusual to the nose and changed perfume when they swayed from one direction to the other. Looking closer at the flower, Petra noticed that each one housed a tiny little fairy creature. The fairies were nothing Petra had seen before. They had, two, red and white spotted horns on their heads, ones that glowed in the dark, chubby cheeks which suited their round faces, and eyelashes that seemed longer than the hair on their head.

As one of them turned away a curly tail sticking out at the base of their backs wiggled. The fairies seemed to be nurturing the pods of pollen that sat in the centre of the petal bases. Petra bent down further for a closer look. The little creatures smiled at her, then continued to stroke the globules of dust as if getting them off to sleep. The field skirted around the base of a beautiful palace that stood proud in the distance on top of a mountain.

"I've arranged for my unicorns to take you up to the palace. It is easy to forget that not everything has wings," Mardy laughed and walked them over to the beautiful white unicorns. "If you have never ridden one before it's easy, just sit back and relax."

All four unicorns knelt on their front legs and lowered their heads. Mardy helped all but Aster onto their backs. When all four had mounted, the unicorns stood up and stretched out their wings. The wings stretched almost double the length of the unicorns' bodies and a pale golden dust evaporated out as they opened. The wings flapped slowly lifting them into the air. Louie guessed that Aster had done this before: he looked natural. Mardy led the way without a unicorn.

Louie was fascinated by the beautiful creature he was riding. He stroked its mane; the hair was a multitude of pale pastel colours that glistened like diamonds. The horn on its head looked like frosted glass and the hair on its body was as soft as the clouds. Louie put his arms around its neck and hugged it as they flew, enjoying the warm night air rush against his face.

Mardy was the first to land in the courtyard of the palace followed by Aster scoring a perfect landing. Louie, Petra and Juggle relied on their unicorns to land and stop without help. Once again the unicorns were kind and lowered back onto their knees allowing each rider the chance to slide off. Which was exactly what they did.

Mardy and Aster didn't stop talking from the moment they landed until they entered the Great Room in the palace. It was an astonishing room full of golden furniture, platinum walls and a crushed diamond white floor.

Louie, Petra and Juggle, gasping as they entered, were breathtaken at the sight. Mardy walked over to a long crystal curtain that hung on one of the walls.

He pulled it back and opened up a doorway to a hidden room that looked less spectacular than the last.

"This is my thinking room," Mardy said proudly, "I had to have somewhere that wasn't so sparkling bright. I have your uncle to blame for that, Louie. Too many years playing in caves trying to plan the pretend attacks against the underworld, my eyes took a while to adapt when I eventually came back to Verlum. I definitely think easier when not surrounded by the beautiful blinding sparkles of the palace.'

Louie looked around the room; it was very understated in comparison. dark old leather-bound books covered two of the walls. The ceiling in this room was lower than the Great Room. It had a single purple velvet curtain hanging at a full-length window next to an old wooden dining table. On the opposite side of the room stood a rocking chair padded out with tatty old cushions that sat next to a small round table. The room was tidy, but well used.

"Please take a seat at the table. I have asked that we have some food and drink brought in. That way we know no one else can hear what we are talking about."

The five of them sat and ate at the table listening to Aster and Mardy's tales of when they were young. Louie hadn't heard much about his uncle's childhood. It was good to see him relaxing without the weight of the world literally on his shoulders.

# Gods and Angels United

"Mardy, the reason I have brought Louie and his friends along with me is because Louie made a very good point. He has suggested that we find out as much about Es'trixia's magic as we can. If it's her magic being used to win them the scroll and power over our worlds there may be a key to it that will allow us to overpower her. We know Onyx lived in your world and we wondered if you would have any objection to Louie finding out what he can about the magic and, hopefully, the key to stopping it."

Mardy looked at Louie and then at Aster. "It would be a great honour to have help from Tarania and a good thought by you, Louie. I think you may be right. This could be our only chance at playing her and Julique at their own game. We only have one cycle until the eclipse so I think it would be wise for me to send three of my very knowledgeable students along with you. It will save time and you can then concentrate on the matter in hand rather than trying to find your way about this unfamiliar world on your own. Also youngsters would never be suspected by Julique.

"I will let you rest your heads tonight and when you wake in the morning all will be in place for you." Mardy looked at Aster and stood up from the table. "Aster shall we take a walk? I think we need to discuss our plan. We will be very busy until the eclipse."

Mardy called the pixie back into the room and explained that they would have guests staying the night. Aster and Mardy left the small room and strolled out of sight, deep in conversation.

"This is so exciting Louie," Juggle said. "No wonder you couldn't say anything to us. This is big, really big. You're going to have to explain who Onyx is? I can't say I've ever heard of her and what is this Extrix magic?"

"The magic is called Es'trixia," Petra corrected, "and it is called this because the witch that conjured the magic is called Es'trixia. She is a very evil, powerful witch. Onyx on the other hand was one of three sisters that were born into the first Light and dark blood family. They were known as 'the sisters' by the elders and were the first to have the mixture of both bloods. You must have heard of the angel Julique?"

"Sure," Juggle said, shuddering at the thought, "my dad would tell me bedtime stories about the bad things he did to the angel world."

"Bedtime sounds a barrel of laughs in your house," Louie scoffed, nudging Juggle in the ribs.

"Well," Petra continued, "he was against the mixing of light and dark blood. Julique believed it was too powerful a combination that would allow the gods to take over the light of the angels and rule them, and eventually create an evil that couldn't be controlled. He was obviously wrong because the mix of the bloods was even better for creation and proved that the blood mix made no difference by turning evil himself. Onyx on the other hand was wonderful."

"How do you know so much about this? I don't remember this being taught in class," Juggle asked whilst turning to Louie for agreement.

"My mum made me have extra tutoring on the history of witches and magic. She said that it was part of my heritage and I should 'know the old in order to improve the new'. One of the subjects was history of the dark and light blood sisters. I found Onyx the most interesting because she made it her life's work to find Es'trixia and dissect her magic with the intention of using it for good rather than evil."

"So what happened to her?" Juggle asked.

"Nobody knows. After the sisters went their separate ways, they started new lives under different names because Julique hunted them and wanted them dead. Even though they weren't known by their true identities, history says it was easy to tell who they were, because they had beautiful auras of goodness that couldn't be hidden."

"So Onyx could've been killed by Es'trixia?'

"That's what's thought to have happened. Onyx went on a search for Es'trixia and never returned to where it is thought she lived. Sad, isn't it? To think of her out there on her own wanting to overcome the most evil magic and she was killed without any of her sisters knowing for sure. So, Louie, what's the plan?" Petra asked, folding her arms and looking at Louie.

"I thought it'd be an idea to go to where Onyx lived and look for anything that relates to Es'trixia's magic. It's a long shot but we don't have much more to go on. She must have left something in her house. P, do you think there might be a way to stop the evil magic?"

"I was taught that in order to conjure evil magic a part of it had to be from good magic, otherwise the power would be too weak. So in answer to your question you would have to know what part of the magic was good and what part was evil and, to know that, you would have to see the book of magic it came from."

"In other words unless we can get to Es'trixia's book of magic we are not going to find out?"

"Maybe. We will have to see what Onyx managed to find out. You're right, Louie, if anyone would know it would've been Onyx. Let's hope we find where she lived first and then see if anything was left there."

The pixie that served their food earlier entered the room. Looking at the three visitors from over the top of her half-moon glasses she beckoned them through the door.

"Young ones, please follow. Your beds are ready," she snapped.

The little pixie walked quickly along the long hallway, snapping her wings every few steps and simultaneously lifting her feet off the ground at the same time, flying in between steps. The three friends followed behind her until they reached a spiral staircase.

"Make your way up the stairs and you will find your beds. Belongings have been taken up already. I will wake you at morning light. You don't have long, young ones, so I would hurry and close your eyes."

Juggle ran up the staircase and leapt onto the first bed he saw. Louie and Petra followed admiring the navy-coloured room that set the mood for sleeping. Louie took his shoes off and lay down on his bed on top of the soft feather blanket.

"Look at the stars above us. Have you ever seen them so clearly?" Petra lay on her back amazed at the sight of the sky through the glass ceiling above her. "They all look so close to the ground in this world."

Louie drifted off to sleep listening to his best friend discuss the different stars above them. Soon they were all asleep and the room was silent.

# The Six Seekers of Onyx

At sunrise they were escorted by the same little pixie back into Mardy's thinking room. They sat at the table looking and feeling very tired. Before the three of them had enough time to relax into their chairs Mardy and Aster entered looking very awake. Following behind them were three other 'beings' they hadn't met before.

"Morning," Mardy said cheerfully, "I hope you slept well and feel ready to fight the day ahead." He smiled as he looked at the tired faces of the three youngsters sitting slumped at the table.

"Breakfast will be here in a flash and you will feel wide awake after that. Meanwhile I would like to introduce your Verlum guides that will accompany you to wherever it is you wish to go."

Mardy stepped to one side allowing the three beings, from behind, to step forward. He introduced each individually. "First we have Summer, my daughter, she will be your guide along the journey."

Louie felt himself blush at the sight of the beautiful angel girl standing in front of him. Her hair was platinum blonde and turquoise and her face was the prettiest he had ever seen. It was her ice-blue eyes and welcoming smile that made his heart skip a beat.

Mardy raised his voice jumping Louie out of his stare. Then we have Squidge and Tia, they are Summer's closest friends and my best students. I know you are all going to get along just fine."

Everyone said hello to one another and settled down to their breakfast whilst discussing the best method to get to Dazlum, the village that Onyx was thought to have lived.

"It is decided then. You will take three unicorns and ride them in pairs," Mardy said finishing his toasted sugar bread.

"Are you all prepared, Louie?' asked Aster. 'We can only hope you find something out. We will be making other plans at our end in case nothing is found."

Everyone stood up from the table and headed to the court yard to meet the unicorns.

Aster gave Louie a manly hug and wished him and his friends luck in their search. Mardy was gentler with his team of helpers, kissing his daughter and Tia on their forehead and stroking Squidge's velvety ears as he said his goodbyes.

Before they knew it the six seekers of Onyx were on their way into the sky on the back of the unicorns once again. Louie was ecstatic when he was told he would be riding the same unicorn as Summer. He thought she was the most beautiful angel he'd ever seen. Squidge rode with Juggle, and Petra shared with Tia.

"How long will the journey to Dazlum take?" Louie shouted to Summer, fighting the wind rush.

"We should be there by dusk. It may be a thought to stop and camp out close to the village tonight. I don't know what we are going to find when we get there. What I've read about Dazlum suggests there is not much more than a small village there, but it's better to approach the unknown in daylight, I find."

Louie's tummy jumped with nervous excitement at the thought of being so close to Summer throughout the whole journey. She was intelligent, beautiful and enjoyed an adventure. Louie's ideal girl.

"How comes your father sent you to help us?" asked Louie.

"My father strongly believes that if you are in line to rule the land, you should know the land you will be ruling. Any adventure to discover different parts of our world and father jumps at the chance to send Squidge, Tia and me. We love the experience and the challenge. Many royals are kept close to the palace. I'm just glad I'm not one of them. I think I would suffocate if I couldn't explore."

"Have you been to many places far away?"

"I have been to many places but nowhere as far away as we're going. This is a true adventure; there may be danger when we get there and most of all we actually have a purpose to explore."

"Aren't you afraid of what we might find when we get there? What if Julique has found out we're looking for a magic to stop him? He will kill us."

"Louie, you must never be afraid of what hasn't happened until it happens. You should have faith that you can tackle anything that's thrown at you. Sometimes things work out better if you don't overthink them.

"You can only plan so far in advance whilst on adventures. Julique may have already been to this area and tricked someone from our world into doing what he wants. If he can't get his minions into Verlum he will have to recruit from within. That's why we must be careful who we trust along the way."

Louie thought for a while, taking in all that Summer said. He liked her outlook on life and she was right. Why worry about something that hasn't happened? It was silly to waste unnecessary energy that could be used elsewhere. He relaxed some more and soaked in the setting sun on the horizon, the warmth on his face made him close his eyes and smile and, as he did so, his hold around Summer followed his feelings of total warmth and relaxation. He made himself jump when he realised his grip was getting firmer around Summer's waist as if hugging her. Louie's face turned scarlet with embarrassment. Summer on the other hand didn't mind but kindly ignored it to save embarrassment.

The unicorns were gliding at a comfortable height now, their wings still smoothly riding the air current keeping the riders still as they did so. On looking down at the land below, the colours were emerald green and the lakes sapphire blue. They were riding at such a height, the villages they passed overlooked like small specks of paint accidentally spilt on a painting.

"How long have you known your friends?" asked Louie, not having to shout over the wind any more.

"We grew up together. Squidge is a creation called a scruffin."

"My father mentioned scruffins. Aren't they magical helpers to the elders?"

"Yes. Squidge is the first to ever live away from the elders' table. Both my father's parents were elders when I was born and as a birth present they sent me my own scruffin, who was only little herself. We have done everything together from that day on. I love her so much." Summer turned her head back to face the direction they were going in.

"How about Tia? I'm guessing she's a pixie?"

"Tia is actually a mix of pixie and angel blood, though she looks more like a pixie. Both her parents died when she was very young and, being good friends of my mother and father, they took her on as their own daughter. I've always treated her as a sister. Tia is very wise when she has to be, but most of the time she's mischievous, always playing tricks and games. Sometimes I find it hard to take her seriously at all. She is lots of fun. Typical pixie!"

"That sounds very similar to Juggle. He is a mix of angel and fairy blood; he's good fun too."

"Petra has a very soothing aura about her."

"P is a great friend. She knows what you're thinking before you do. Very intuitive, and she does actually make you feel calm when you're around her. P is a healing witch."

"A witch? That is fascinating. I keep a journal of all creations I meet. I can't wait to talk to Petra and find out everything I can about her."

Summer and Louie continued to talk about their friends for the rest of the journey exchanging stories of school and the adventures they had experienced. The unicorns continued flying until dusk settled across the sky, eventually landing at the edge of a forest Summer had read about, not too far from where they were heading.

Tia and Juggle hit it off straight away, laughing and joking whilst looking for firewood. Tia hid behind trees jumping out on Juggle causing him to fall over every time with fright. Summer and Petra found a good place for them all to shelter for the night and made a roof of leaves over some tree stumps, whilst Louie and Squidge looked for soft foliage to use for their bedding.

Squidge was as cute as his father had described scruffins to be. She was short with the cutest of faces, her eyes were wide and blue, her nose was black and her soft white velvet ears flopped to her cheeks. Louie couldn't believe the softness of her fur, it was as if there was nothing there when he touched her. The fur was pure white with a pale pink tinge on her tummy. Squidge had small, chiffony wings yet somehow furry on her back, finished off with ball of fluff for a tale. Louie thought himself lucky to see a scruffin let alone be with one on his journey.

Once Tia and Juggle had found enough firewood to keep them warm, they made a fire and settled into the shelter Summer and Petra had made. Squidge and Louie arranged the bedding on the ground allowing all six to lay in a line, side by side, sharing cloaks to keep warm. Louie felt it was his duty to look after the smallest of the group so he snuggled Squidge into the crook of his armpit making sure she was covered with his cloak.

"What do you think will happen, Squidge?"

"I don't know, I am scared though, aren't you? If Julique becomes as powerful as we think he might, the worlds will be in turmoil. We must find something to stop him."

The six new friends drifted off to sleep under their self-made shelter huddled together.

Louie hadn't slept long enough to dream before he felt someone nudging his shoulder. Still feeling too sleepy to open his eyes, Louie ignored the first few nudges he felt before the nudging became harder; he slowly remembered where he was.

"Louie?" whispered Squidge, "Louie wake up. I think there's something in the trees." Squidge put her furry little paw to Louie's mouth, stopping him from making a noise. The fire had smouldered to a soft orange glow of embers so it was hard to see into the thick black air. Squidge placed a pair of tiny spectacles on the bridge of Louie's nose making the night air look like dusk; he could just make out an outline of something moving in the distance.

"What is it?" quizzed Louie quietly.

"I don't know, but whatever it is I think it has been in the bushes for a while. There is a stench coming from that direction, that's what woke me up."

Louie took a sniff of the air. "Awgul stench," Louie whispered screwing his nose up. "I saw awguls in the tunnel yesterday."

"I have never seen this creature in Verlum before. I better wake Summer," Squidge said, crawling to where Summer was sleeping. Keeping as low to the ground as possible, she gently shook Summer's shoulder. Summer opened her eyes and saw Squidge in front of her with her finger to her lips.

"What is it, Squidge?" Summer whispered, knowing it must be important.

"There's something in the bushes. Louie says it smells like an awgul but I have never known them in our world before." Summer took the tiny spectacles from Louis and looked through them. Squidge was correct there was something perched in a bush directly ahead of their camp. The creature had piercing green eyes.

"Do you think it's watching us?"

"Maybe," answered Summer, "but whatever it is they wouldn't know who we are or why we're here. If Julique has managed to get his creatures into Verlum, without the army being warned, I'm guessing he wants something that Onyx had. There's nothing around to bring anyone else to these parts." Summer handed the spectacles back to Squidge.

"We should stay quiet until the awgul thing has gone in the chance he doesn't know we're here. We need to cover our tracks tomorrow." Summer, Squidge and Louie woke the others, still at a whisper, and told them what had happened. The new camp of friends drifted back to sleep listening to every little sound the woods made, aware something could well be watching them.

The next morning, after a very non-exciting breakfast of bread and honey, the companions decided it would be a lot less conspicuous to walk the rest of the journey than to ride the unicorns for all to see.

Before leaving the camp Tia rummaged around in her flower-shaped satchel and pulled out a small dewdrop-shaped bottle. She tipped the bottle over her hand and shook it hard, sprinkling a transparent dust that glimmered as it fell. Tia circled the unicorns throwing the dust into the air around them. When the dust was all gone, she stood back and watched as the veil of glimmering dust melted into a haze landing on the unicorns.

"Why have you done that, Tia? Have you cast a spell?" asked Petra intrigued at what she had just seen.

"No spells have been cast. I've sprinkled pixie dust over the unicorns to cover them up while we're gone. The dust will camouflage the unicorns to all eyes apart from ours. To us it will look like I have placed a haze over them, but to anyone else they will just see the fields and flowers that surround them as if the unicorns aren't here." Tia brushed her hands together removing any residue of pixie dust. "As long as the three of them can keep quiet no one will ever know they are here." All three unicorns bowed to Tia to say thank you. Tia smiled back. "You're welcome."

Dazlum was shown on Summer's map on the opposite edge of the forest to where they were. They all planned the route they would take and this was straight through the centre of the forest.

Trundling off into the forest the group clambered over fallen trees and pushed their way through thick prickly hedges. For a while Juggle and Louie stayed towards the back and tried their best to cover any obvious tracks that showed they'd been there.

It wasn't long before they could see sunlight through the trees ahead encouraging a quicker pace to what they assumed was the edge of the forest, when in fact it was not the edge at all.

# Zinkas

Louie and Juggle were the first to break through the last line of trees, and when they did, their eyes were hit by a mesmerizing sun-kissed sparkling pool surrounded by the most brightly coloured flowers they had ever seen. It was as if a rainbow had beamed down from the sky and hit the petals of every flower giving them an intense injection of colour. Following close behind, Summer, Petra, Squidge and Tia were stopped instantly in their tracks, when they too laid eyes on the beautiful flowers.

A little further on, into this oasis of colour, Juggle and Louie started to experience something strange. Both of them became light on their feet and felt all their energy seep from their limbs. They were being lifted into the air and carried towards the pool in front of them.

"Louie?" Juggle said in a slow woozy voice, unable to use his mouth properly, 'do you feel strange? I can't feel my body any more. What's happening?" Louie didn't answer.

Juggle used all of his might, turning his head to the side, to see where Louie was. All he could see was Louie flying towards the pool. Then something caught his eye. There was some sort of creature hovering around Louie. Juggle's eyes were getting sleepy now and he was finding it hard to keep them open.

"Just one more look," he tried telling himself out loud. Juggle managed to open one eye fully and the other only slightly, again seeing something hovering around Louie. Juggle's mind paused, then his eyes translated what he'd seen. The deadly realisation hit Juggle and it was as if he had been hit in the face.

"Zinka fairies!" he shrieked in the loudest mumble he could produce. Juggle tried as hard as he could to shake his body. It was slow at first but gradually he started to feel himself gain control. The numb feeling was fading fast and he was getting closer to the ground. He landed with a thud on the ground, bottom first, crumpling his wings.

Within a matter of seconds, and not realising the pain he was in, he was up off the ground running towards Louie. Louie was now lying flat in mid-air over the pool.

"Louie!" shouted Juggle in his loudest voice, "Louie wake up!" Juggle was never panicked but right now this was an extreme panic of life or death.

The zinka fairies were now attacking Juggle as he shouted at Louie. He fought them off the best he could but he couldn't risk touching the pool.

Juggle had only heard tales of zinka fairies and the spell pool. The spell pool sat in the centre of the flower garden surrounded by all the wonder of the mesmerizing flowers and foliage. A water fountain sat in the middle that sprayed clear turquoise water continuously back into the pool creating a serene sound of calm, adding to the addictive staying power. The tales Juggle had heard were that any male beings that came into contact with the spell pool would be trapped within it forever with no way out. Zinka fairies lived only around these pools and enticed their prey in by the colours of the flowers and the relaxing sensation of the pool.

Juggle knew that he couldn't risk flying over the pool; his wings were too damaged and he could cause them both to be swallowed. He looked around frantically for the others.

The four girls stood by a beautiful green bush of blue flowers admiring each individual flower by smell. Juggle knew they'd been mesmerized and he didn't have long to snap them out of it before Louie was gone forever.

Still fighting off a swarm of zinkas, Juggle summersaulted purposely towards the girls, crash landing into them. Knocking all four girls off their feet, each girl seemed startled and shook their head. Juggle grabbed Squidge and Tia under his arm and ran them to the edge of the pool. "They both have wings," he thought out loud, "they can fly to him."

"Get him down without touching the water," he shouted to them.

Squidge and Tia felt they were moving in slow motion as they watched the zinkas let go of Louie's body. They were too late.

"Nooooo...!" Juggle screamed watching his best friend plummet towards the surface of the pool.

In the same breath Summer had gained consciousness and flew at speed in between Juggle and Tia. As fast as she could, she reached out to Louie as he fell. Angling herself, she hit Louie in his side pushing him across to the other side of the pool. At the same time Tia and Squidge had launched themselves besides her as extra help to fight off the zinkas who had tried to make a wall in front of Louie.

Juggle sprinted round to the other side of the spell pool as fast as he could.

"We need to get away from here now!" shouted Juggle.

The commotion of the zinkas was loud and frantic. They were like piranhas with wings. Juggle hoisted Louie over one shoulder without giving him a chance to walk or even fathom out what was happening. Juggle and the girls ran for their lives towards the other side of the forest edge, being chased by very angry zinka fairies. They all dived over the grass line that separated the spell pool from the forest, and watched as the zinkas hit an invisible wall that stopped them from following. The zinkas were angry, staying at the wall snarling and snapping their teeth.

Some of the zinkas continued to fly at the wall with anger.

Summer, Squidge and Tia ran to Juggle and Petra, who had landed further away with Louie in tow.

"Louie. Are you OK?" Petra slapped his cheeks to get some response. A moment passed and he started to come round. Louie drowsily pulled himself to a sitting position, resting his back up against a tree and his elbows on his knees. He rubbed his head with both hands.

"What in Druce's name just happened? Why do I feel I've just fought my uncle's army single handed?"

Juggle chuckled; thankful his friend was not face down in the pool for eternity. "Louie," Juggle said, throwing his arms around Louie and hugging him hard, "that was really close, mate. We nearly lost you."

"We nearly lost both of you," Petra added joining in on the hug. Before Louie could push them off, Squidge, Tia and Summer piled on top and they all hugged Louie. All six started laughing with relief. They had survived the zinka fairies.

As Juggle rolled onto his back, he winced. "Ouch!" he yelped, forgetting he'd crumpled his wings after falling from a great height.

"Juggle. What's wrong?" Tia picked herself off the floor and walked around to Juggle's back. She looked at his wings. "Oh dear, your wings... they look... ummm, how can I put it? Broken!"

Tia knelt down and tried to figure out what had and hadn't broken. Tia called Squidge over. "Squidge. Do you have any diamond ointment with you?" Squidge opened the pouch she carried around her tummy and picked out a small glass pot. She handed the pot to Tia and watched Tia unscrew the lid. Scooping some of the contents out Tia handed the pot back to Squidge and warmed the ointment in her palms. Placing her hands on Juggle's wings she gently dabbed the ointment onto the broken areas, leaving a golden residue on the areas her hands had touched.

"They feel warm," Juggle said trying to stand himself up.

"Just sit for a while, the ointment will help heal your wings but you must give it a chance."

"Wings take ages to heal, Tia. One time it took them a whole school term. I missed out on all the sports races. I was so bored."

"With this ointment dabbed on them they will feel better in no time. They won't heal straight away but by sundown you'll see a huge difference." Tia wrapped bandages around the worst part of the wings, hoping they heal back into their original shape.

"What happened back there?" Louie asked. He was back to normal now and concerned about Juggle's wings. Louie peered over Tia's shoulder and watched as she mended his wings.

"Have you ever heard of zinka fairies?" Juggle replied, looking over his shoulder at Louie trying to keep his wings as still as he could for Tia.

"No. Never."

"Well," Juggle started. "Zinkas, as you saw, are nasty evil little fairies. They were conjured as a form of protection against people that wanted to steal magic, back in the days that the angels and gods were at war. The spell pools were placed in an area that would have to be passed in order to reach the magic and only work on male beings. This was in anticipation of Julique hunting for their magic. Women are mesmerized by the smells and colours of the flowers.

"At first you're hit by the dazzling beauty of the spell pool, then the zinkas pounce, sinking their teeth into the skin of their prey. Their needle-sharp teeth release a paralyzing poison into the skin; your energy is drained instantly putting you deep into an unconscious daze. When you're at this point, they take you to the centre of the spell pool and float you in mid-air. Once the pool is ready to receive its prey, the zinkas drop you into the water, trapping you in there for all eternity. The spell pool expands with every victim it takes also increasing the number of zinkas. You were very lucky, Louie. If it wasn't for Summer—"

Louie interrupted Juggle. "What do you mean if it wasn't for Summer?"

"Summer flew to you as you were falling towards the water. She managed to push you away from the pool before you touched the water." Louie felt himself blush at the thought of being saved by a girl.

"It wasn't just me," Summer added quickly, feeling Louie's awkwardness. "Squidge and Tia were at my side; it was a group effort. If it wasn't for Juggle knocking us girls out of the spell we were under, all of us would be in trouble."

"Shall we get back on our trail now we are all mended?" Petra said eagerly. "It's nearly lunchtime and I think we're close. Looking at the map it's just through those trees." Petra pointed ahead whilst picking her own bag off the floor and putting it on her back. All six continued on through the forest slower than they had done before they were attacked.

Eventually they stepped out from the forest trees and onto a carpet of emerald-green grass fringed with various types of toad stalls, some nearly as tall as Louie. The friends sat down next to the white and yellow toadstools that seemed to stand higher, allowing the group to hide themselves from plain sight, and ate a well-deserved lunch which again was nothing more than stale bread and honey.

# Awguls

Creations that had not been successful in the way the elders had imagined were sent to the underworld. This included awguls. Known for being weak-minded and spiteful, they were used as thieves by most underworld creatures. Awguls were seen as powerless and stupid; they were minions to the evils that lay in the underworld, but as time had gone on the awguls had realised that they needed to gain their own authority in order to be treated with some respect and not used to carry out everyone else's dirty work. Julique used the awguls for all of his dirty work.

The awguls working for Julique had been given the spell by Es'trixia that would help them to step into Verlum undetected. The spell was for a limited time and allowed two awguls to be cloaked.

It was decided by the head awgul which two would be sent. The chosen two were given a green vile of liquid to drink whilst the spell was being cast. Finishing the vile and spell at the same time, the chosen two vanished into thin air and out of Julique's lair. Within seconds they landed in a bush amongst some trees. Darkness had fallen so they had to use their green eyes to see in the dark.

Awguls all looked the same: short, fat bodies with coarse wiry brown hair in patches all over. Their noses were snout-like and most of the time dripping with green snot. Their eyes changed colour from green at night to black during the day. Awguls ate whatever they could find, normally small insects and worms dug up from the soil with their long fingers.

They smelt as if they never cleaned themselves, which they didn't, and would leave a stench lingering everywhere they went. There was nothing particularly nice about awguls at all. They were really stupid too.

The two chosen awguls were called Rog and Dip. They were younger than most of the group and knew they couldn't return to the underworld empty handed.

"Rog?" Dip snorted from the bush they had landed in. "Look light over dare. Wot Is it?" Dip was the younger of the two and looked to Rog as a mentor.

"Fire," Rog replied in his usual stroppy and 'too much effort' tone.

"Shall I go see why dare's fire?"

"Don't bover," Rog shrugged, "looks like camp, wood folk or somfing, nuffin for us to take, gotta stay low and do wot been sent to do. Dare's not much time. Weel wait 'ere case wee've been seen den go village."

"OK," Dip said staying crouched. Seeing no movement from where the fire was dimly lit, Rog and Dip left the bush and scurried into the forest towards the village where Onyx once lived.

Little did they know that they had been spotted by a scruffin.

# Dazlum

Once they'd eaten lunch Louie and his friends got onto an overgrown path on the other side of the meadow. Without warning Tia's feet dramatically slipped from beneath her.

"Yuck! What is that?" Tia looked at her feet and saw she had landed in gooey green slime. She picked herself up and brushed the dirt from her pretty lilac dress. Petra gave Tia a helping hand and investigated the green stain.

"Awguls' slime," Petra said.

"It stinks," Tia complained. "I'll be smelt before I'm seen."

"Never," Juggle added. "You'll always be heard before you're seen or," chuckled Juggle, "you will now be heard before you're smelt."

Forgetting that his wings were healing, Tia ran over to him and slopped a big handful of the slime on his back.

"Now that's funny," Tia giggled.

Everyone laughed until Louie realised what this meant. "Hey, this is bad. This confirms that Julique has managed to get awguls into Verlum. He must want something from Onyx too. We have to hurry.

We must get to the village before they do. Let's hope they're too slow and stupid to get there sooner than us."

The group picked up their pace and ran following Juggle who used a stick to hack away the overgrown brambles that restricted the path. They headed towards a spire seen in the distance.

"I remember reading about the spire in Dazlum. Onyx, supposedly, lived not far from it," puffed Petra.

A rough and uneven cobbled path greeted the friends, allowing them to run a bit quicker. Petra was astonished at how busy the village was. In her imagination, she had expected it to be a quiet soulless place, but it was far from it. The path led into the centre of the village from what she could make out. They were in luck, she thought to herself. A crowd of marketgoers filled the area. Petra led the way, weaving in and out of the crowd until she spotted the spire to her right and quickly chose the path with the most bushes along it. She gave instructions to stay low and the friends followed, taking the right-hand fork in the path. Trying to stay inconspicuous, they picked up their pace once again until they reached the spire set on top of a water well next to a quaint stream.

"This way," whispered Petra pointing to a small rickety wooden bridge leading over the stream. "Her cottage was on the other side of this stream. I remember reading that she sometimes sat by the stream writing spells."

When they reached the bridge Petra continued to lead the way crossing in single file. The stream was crystal clear showing the fish that swam within and the rockery at the bottom. The bustle of the busy village was now a dull murmur in the background. No one was in this part of the village and, by the looks of it, no one had been out this way in a while.

The cottage next to the stream looked old and unloved. It sat alone with ivy growing all over and wild flowers covering the vacant areas in front. The rear of the cottage sat on the stream; the front faced onto a meadow that stretched out to the horizon.

They crept down the side of the cottage towards the front, then stood and listened for movement inside. There was nothing but silence until a bird started to sing its cheery tune in the distance. The friends looked at one another unsure of what to do.

Suddenly there was an almighty crashing sound from within the cottage. All six jumped on the spot with fright. Louie, being the quickest to react, turned to the group and pointing to Juggle and Tia first he indicated for them to go to the back of the cottage and for Squidge and Summer to stay where they were, nearest the side window. He looked at Petra suggesting for her to follow him to the front door, whispering to them all before splitting up, "Stay alert. Awguls are spiteful." Each pair crept off.

Louie and Petra stood with their ears to the front door. There was silence again. Louie's heart was thudding in his chest. Petra put her hand on his shoulder. For a split second Louie thought this was to calm him down, until Petra kicked the front door as hard as she could, causing it to fly off its rotting hinges and land in the hallway.

"AGGGGHHHH!" Louie shouted in shock, caught off guard by Petra's sudden burst of bravery. Petra jumped over the fallen door and landed towards the back of the hallway. Making himself stay put, Louie hurriedly scanned the area. Something moved from the corner of his eye. He turned and saw a small, fat hairy figure jump into the room on his left.

Louie instantly drew the dagger from his belt and crept towards the room. The floor creaked as he moved. The stench was unbearable. Louie reached the doorway and stopped. Knowing that awguls were short he quickly held the dagger above his head and slid it around the top corner of the doorway. Holding it at an angle, pointing the blade downwards, he could see the awgul crouched in a position ready to pounce. The awgul's slime made a squelching noise as it dripped from its nose onto the floor. Louie, knowing he would have to fight, ran into the room intending to tackle the awgul by tying its own cloak around its body restricting all movement, but this didn't go according to plan at all.

As Louie ran into the room he slipped on a pool of slime placed at the door by Rog. Hitting the floor with his entire body, and banging his head at the same time, he dropped his dagger. Rog jumped on him immediately. Louie managed to get his arms in between them both, creating some distance from his face and Rog's long, sharp green claws that were trying to gouge his eyes out.

Rog was persistent; he pushed the full weight of his fat hairy body onto Louie, getting closer to his face with his stubby arms until he scored.

Rog managed to gouge a lump of flesh out of Louie's cheek, grinning, he continued to aim for the eyes.

Louie screamed in pain and the reaction to the pain added an intense surge of power to his arms. He managed to throw Rog off himself causing him to fall back and hit his head on a table positioned against the wall. Louie stretched out his arm, and attempted to reach for the dagger on the far side of the room.

"Not close enough," he panicked.

As he scrambled his feet together to push himself along the floor to get closer, Rog grabbed his leg and snapped his sharp pointy teeth towards his ankle trying to bite. Using his free leg, Louie kicked his foot as hard as he could into Rog's snout. Rog let out a high-pitched squeal buying Louie enough time to grab his dagger and stumble to his feet.

Momentarily Louie hesitated. If he wanted to live he would have to fight the awgul to the death. Louie ran at Rog, who was now back in his crouching position. Holding his dagger in the air Louie was ready to plunge it into Rog's stubby body but, as Louie reached forward, Rog dashed to the opposite side of the room and to the door. Rog looked back towards Louie. Rog knew that he had two options: stay and fight, even though his nose injury had caused him to lose most of his eyesight, or run away and return later if the cloaking spell allowed enough time. Decision made. Rog darted out the door.

Louie was tired. *Where are the others?* he thought. Picking himself off the floor Louie followed Rog out the door. A slime trail led to the front and continued around the side of the cottage towards the stream. Louie saw Rog running towards the bridge. Thinking quickly, he pulled the staff his father had given him from his cloak. Aiming at Rog, Louie hurled the staff, like a spear, hitting Rog on his back causing him to stumble over the top of the bridge and into the stream. Rog screeched again in a high-pitched tone but this time the screech didn't stop. Louie ran over to where Rog had fallen off the bridge and witnessed him disintegrating into a green mist of smelly gas, leaving nothing but a cloak resting on the surface of the water. Louie felt bad; he'd never hurt anything before today and he didn't intend to kill the awgul.

Summer and Squidge ran to join Louie on the bridge. The three of them peered down into the water.

"Louie what happened? We couldn't get to you. Was that the awgul?" asked Summer.

"Yes it was." Louie ran back over the bridge and onto the bank where his staff lay. He picked it up and turned to Summer. "Where are the other three?" As he waited for Summer to answer a howl was heard from the back of the cottage. The three ran around to the rear garden and were met by Tia, Petra and Juggle circling another awgul that had been tied to a chair. They stopped abruptly relieved to see that no one from their group was being hurt.

"Who sent you?" Tia shouted, stopping in front of the awgul. Dip snarled and spat slime at Tia, hitting her on the foot.

"You disgusting little cretin." Tia shook her foot hoping the stench would ease if there wasn't so much slime on her. It didn't work.

Juggle patted Dip's cloak down from behind knowing he couldn't be spat at from behind. Dip struggled in his chair trying to stop the search of his cloak.

Juggle stopped when he reached the lower inside pocket of the cloak.

"Well, well, well. What is this?" Juggle questioned smugly, as he pulled out a roll of parchment tied together with ribbon and a short spear of mirrored glass.

Dip tried to turn his head towards Juggle, attempting to bite whatever he could get hold of. Juggle jumped back further just in case. He placed the mirrored spear on the floor and unrolled the parchment revealing a blank page.

"Why do you want this? It's blank."

Dip snarled again, not answering. Juggle carried on searching the cloak. There was nothing.

"What do we do with him?" asked Juggle. "If we let him go he will run and tell Julique we're here!"

Dip started to struggle in his chair again, this time trying to tip it off balance.

After the group had stood silent for a while thinking of their options, watching as Dip tried to push the chair over, Summer spoke, "Why don't P and Louie go back into the cottage and have a proper look inside? The awguls may have a blank piece of parchment but they also may have missed something." Petra and Louie nodded. "We'll keep the awgul tied up and by the time you get back we may have an idea of what to do with him," Summer added.

Once in the cottage Petra and Louie began their search in the study. The room was untidy with parchment scattered everywhere. Books filled the walls from top to bottom and in the corner of the room sat a desk with more books, parchment sheets and an inkpot, that had tipped over leaving a dark ink stain. Petra ran her finger along the spines of some books that stood upright in the bookcase; the books were mainly about potions and remedies.

"How do we know what we are looking for P?" asked Louie.

"I'm not sure yet. The books on the shelves are just reference books. I've found nothing yet that relates to Es'trixia's magic or the work of Onyx herself. By the look of the room this is where she worked; everything has sat here for so long the cobwebs and dust hide the titles." Petra brushed the cobwebs away from the top shelf. "I can't figure out why there are so many pieces of blank parchment scattered around, you would think with this many blank pages there would be a stack of pieces written on, wouldn't you?"

"Maybe she put them somewhere safe, just in case?"

"Good thought, let's looks for secret hiding places."

The two of them carried on searching the cottage and were getting nowhere fast. Time was ticking and if they didn't find anything the hope of stopping the magic would be gone. Louie looked out the back door to check on the others, who had now been watching the awgul for quite some time. Dusk air was settling across the meadow and they were all looking tired.

As Louie stared at his friends, something bright caught his eye in the sky behind them. He watched as a bright light hurtled towards the cottage at speed

"Look out!" Louie shouted to the others.

All of them quickly turned around in the direction Louie was pointing and witnessed the ball of light hit the ground on the other side of the stream near to the spire.

Tia and Summer ran across the bridge to where the light landed. They were seen to lift something off the ground and carry it over the bridge. Squidge joined them as they stepped off the bridge and helped with the bundle. Juggle stood intrigued but didn't want to take his eye of the awgul.

"What is it, Summer?" asked Juggle from a distance.

"It's a scruffin. I think it might be new; his landing wasn't the best I've seen." Summer laid the scruffin on the floor near to the stream and splashed some water onto his fluffy little cheeks.

Instantly the scruffin sat bolt upright.

"I did it again," he mumbled under his breath rubbing his head at the same time. "Why can't I get it right?"

Squidge leant over the scruffin and wiped water droplets off his nose. "Hello," Squidge said, "are you OK? You took quite a tumble there. My name is Squidge. What's yours?"

"I know who you are. You're the only scruffin ever to live away from the elders' table."

Squidge smiled at him and nodded.

"I'm Tyke." Tyke put out his paw and shook Squidge's paw. "How do you do?"

Tyke was similar in looks to Squidge, the main difference being the tummy. Where Squidge had pink fur on her tummy Tyke, being a boy, had a very light powder blue. Tyke also wore glasses, magnifying his big blue eyes. They both had the same cute soft voice, but Tyke's was slightly lower in tone.

"Are you OK? You took quite a tumble there, Tyke."

"Yes I know. I've been having trouble landing since I was given these glasses. If I take the glasses off I can't see where I'm going but if I keep them on, when I'm in the sky, the ground seems closer than it actually is. I just haven't quite mastered it yet." Tyke stood up rubbing his bottom.

"What are you doing in Dazlum, Tyke?" Squidge continued.

"I am here to collect some ingredients from Onyx's garden. The elders know what you are here for, they too don't know what Julique and Es'trixia have up their sleeve but they know that you are looking to stop them finding the scroll. They can't interfere with any of their creations and the wrongdoing some cause, but, all I will say is," Tyke leaned in and whispered, "I was asked to specifically collect something from here at this time and on finding you all here that might have been the plan." Tyke straightened himself up and continued. "What have you found so far? I might be able to help?"

Summer told Tyke about their journey so far, explaining the awguls being in the cottage when they arrived and how the one they had caught had a blank piece of parchment in its pocket. Summer also explained how they were now stuck and didn't know what to do with the awgul they'd tied up. Tyke listened intently to every word, then summarized:

"OK, so at the moment you have an awgul you don't know what to do with, that's been sent here by Julique and if he has been given a cloaking potion it will wear off soon, meaning Julique will start to wonder where he is with whatever it is he has been sent here for. You've found a piece of blank parchment? Can I see it?" Juggle handed the parchment to Summer who was within reach without leaving the awgul's side.

Tyke unrolled the parchment and examined it. "Ahh, I see, mmmm…" He then held it up to the fast-setting sun.

The group stood and watched as the blank page came to life. Words and pictures jumped around the page, spreading from the centre out, filling the blank space.

"Wow," Petra said out loud, "I would never have thought of that."

"Me neither," agreed Tia.

"What's happening to the page and how?" Petra asked.

"Well," Tyke began, "Onyx conjured a way of secretly writing letters to the elders that if intercepted could only be read if they knew how to make the ink visible. This was helpful on many an occasion when

Julique would try and steal the letters from the deliverers. Luckily we are a lot faster than he or any of his underworld helpers are. Anyway, in order to read the page it has to be held up to the sun by a creation that does not have any spell concealing it. In other words Julique is somewhere, we don't know where for sure, but it is thought that he is hiding in the underworld. If he is it would be impossible for him to read the parchment because there is no sun there. If he is hiding within one of the three worlds he will be using some kind of spell to hide his identity, again meaning he wouldn't be able to read the parchment."

Petra looked at Louie. "There are pages upon pages of blank parchment scattered all over the cottage, maybe they too have something on them after all. If we're quick we might be able to see what some of them say before the sun disappears."

Louie ran back into the cottage returning with both arms full of parchment rolls wrapped in ribbon. Everyone, apart from Juggle who was still on awgul duty, took what they could and quickly unravelled the parchment whilst stood in a line facing what was left of the sun. The friends stood and watched in amazement as the pages danced to life with drawings and words upon seeing the sun. There was still a pile unseen by the sun but the friends were happy with what they had. They would be ready to do more in the morning.

"As for the awgul," Tyke said walking over to him whilst rummaging around in his tummy bag, "if you don't mind I will send him somewhere he won't be found, until we are ready to release him back into the underworld. It is a place called Limbo." Tyke took a small wooden tube out from his tummy bag and pointed it at Dip.

Dip started shaking with fear. "No... Peease... Not Limbo... Noooo...!"

Tyke pressed the top of the tube and Dim was instantly sucked into the tip of it. Tyke bent down and held the tube to the ground. Pressing the top of the tube once again, a pulse of light shot into the ground.

"All done," Tyke finished.

"Where's he gone?" Summer asked as she investigated the ground where a small hole was left.

"Limbo. It's a place in between our worlds and the underworld. No one would ever want to go there out of choice. The soul is separated from the body and tampered with by the demons of the underworld. The body stays in Limbo floating until it is put back with the soul. It is feared by the evil because they are punished to such a point they beg to die; they relive their worst fears. The good thing about doing this to the awgul is if Julique was to scan around for him the search would show him being in the underworld because his soul is in there. Hopefully Julique will think nothing more than the awguls had failed their task and were too scared to return to him."

"Good plan," Juggle agreed. "I hope I never have to go to Limbo. I would hate to be confronted with my fears. It is bad enough dealing with them on a daily basis." Juggle feared animals that ran fast with long sharp teeth. As a young boy he was chased by a rogue Black Forest lion and came very close to being caught and eaten. Luckily his father was close by at the time and heard the scream. He managed to pick him up and fly him out of harm's reach. It was partly Juggle's fault though; he did disturb the forest lion whist in hibernation. Since that day Juggle had been petrified of anything that resembled the lion.

"What's this?" Tyke asked bending down to the mirrored spear.

"We found it on the awgul," Juggle replied.

"It looks like something I've seen the angels carry at the elders' table. It's used to send messages from land to the elders. Julique was obviously hoping to receive a message. I think it would be wise to take it back in case it gets back into the wrong hands." Tyke shrunk the spear to fit into his bag.

"I think we should all settle for the night in the cottage," Tia suggested.

"Good idea, Tia," agreed Louie, "maybe there is some food in the garden that we can pick for dinner. We can eat before we look at the pages."

Squidge turned to Tyke. "Are you going to stay and eat with us?"

"No I can't. I have to get back to the table with these ingredients. But I will be back in the morning to collect some more. It's a big order, so I will see you then and if I can guide you any more I will." Tyke secured his tummy bag, after filling it with ingredients from the cottage garden, and leapt into the sky. Within seconds the ball of light was gone.

The once blank pages were intriguing. Although very old, the content seemed almost recent as if Onyx had foreseen how the worlds would be so many years on.

The group sat and read through all of the pages they'd managed to hold up to the sun before it disappeared. There were lots of unusual spells written to use against certain evil creatures. None though for Julique or Es'trixia's magic. Even so, Petra scribbled as many down in her book as she could.

"Hey look at this page," Petra said. "It's a map. It starts from here and leads to somewhere called Mr Pinchbeak. What's Mr Pinchbeak do you think?"

"It sounds like a being more than a place," Summer answered. "I'll look back through the pages and see if a Mr Pinchbeak has been mentioned before."

Petra continued, "This page has been written in bold ink. Look." Petra held the page up to the candlelight and it showed the map had been over drawn a few times accentuating the path and words Mr Pinchbeak.

"You're right it does, it's as if it's telling us to follow the trail." Louie was stopped mid conversation by Summer.

"I've found something. It mentions Pinchbeak." Summer lay the page flat on the floor in the middle of their circle and moved the shrinking candle nearer.

The page showed a spell. "Wish once, wish twice, steer the water with winged life. Strike the evil when tide is still. Follow to Mr Pinchbeak who will know all."

"What does that mean?" Louie asked knowing none of them would have a clue.

"We may not know right now," Petra started, "but maybe we have to follow the map to find out."

"Yes," Louie agreed nodding his head with the others, "at the moment we've found nothing that looks as if it will help us. When the sun rises we should check the rest of the pages, then follow the map to this Mr Pinchbeak."

Discussing the map over freshly boiled lemon and mint tea the friends tried to decipher the route laid out in front of them. It showed basic drawings of trees and water. The path was a single ink-drawn line curving from the bottom corner of the map to the middle stopping at a tiny island marked with a dot, titled Mr Pinchbeak.

The conversation continued until midnight when they all gave in to their tiredness and settled down to bed.

It was decided that they would check all the pages against the sun's first light and would read them whilst on their path to Mr Pinchbeak's island.

# Dark Bog

Tyke dropped in as promised before their journey started. He pointed them in the right direction and sent them on their way, wishing them luck.

It seemed a long slog of a journey, and though in Verlum the weather was mainly beautiful and sunny, the area they had entered was untouched by the sun. The friends were led to a boggy river where the sky became black with clouds. Lightning could be seen in the distance.

Summer looked at the map. "This bog seems to be the start of the lake the island is in."

"I don't like the feel of it around here," Petra said putting her cloak on around her shoulders and her hood up. "I'm feeling as if we may be unwanted visitors to the folk that live here."

"I'm feeling that too," Tia agreed, "maybe we should try and get out of here sooner rather than later."

Squidge suggested everyone put their cloaks on, as cover, to protect them against the coming rain, but also to camouflage themselves against creatures that may not want them in their territory.

The ground became thicker and thicker with sludge. Trying to stay on the stepping stones along the perimeter of the bog shore, it was hard to judge a steady one against the ones that sunk.

Tia and Squidge, even though they could have hovered over the ground, decided it would be better if no one saw they could fly so Louie carried Squidge on his back. The bog itself burped and farted bubbles causing explosions of black sludge to hit the shore close to their feet. Tired lanky old willow trees overhung the path, some fallen through age and others looked as if they had been purposely felled by teeth marks around the trunk. The thunder rumbled above and the sky swirled with wind but strangely everything else seemed silent and still with no sign of other life.

"We should get closer together," Juggle suggested with worry in his voice, "this storm is weird. I've only known thunder caused by the anger of the Gods in Tarania and you know that will pass once the anger is over. This, on the other hand, doesn't feel controlled by anything. I don't trust it."

The sky swirled with more and more force making it harder for any of them to walk forward. Louie stopped in front and turned to summer.

"What do we do?" Louie shouted over the noise of wind and thunder, whilst ducking the debris that flew through the air around them.

"I don't know. If we stop we're wasting valuable time. We've got to get to the edge of the lake as soon as we can but I don't want us to get hurt trying to get through this. What does everyone think?" All six huddled onto one large stepping stone.

Tia began, "We need to get out the storm, do we try and speed up or find shelter in the hope it stops soon?"

"I think we should try and carry on," answered Juggle. "This storm may go on for…" Juggle's breath was taken away when suddenly the stepping stone, they were all huddled on, dropped from beneath them. All six screamed as they fell. Descending below the bog, at a fast pace, they managed to grab one another. Louie looked at Juggle, who looked at Petra.

How were they going to get out of this alive? The answer was they probably wouldn't. The big stepping stone was still at their feet stopping Louie from seeing what was to meet them all when they eventually found the end. The hole they were falling down changed from its black bog-type exterior to more of a grey slate look. The stepping stone began to slow down steadily before stopping. The six friends jolted with the unforeseen movement landing on their bums hard. The stone hovered momentarily before changing direction and shooting along a horizontal passage. The six friends looked at one another with worry. Had Julique finally realised what they were doing? Had he found someone from Verlum to help him?

Squidge, still on Louie's back, interrupted his thoughts that were being shared with Petra. "Look, there's a doorway ahead."

The stepping stone stopped with a bump at a round white, cloud-like doorway. Tia put her hand out to touch it and soon snatched it back when the door started to open. Stood on all fours in the doorway were two old fierce-looking dragons. All six stayed silently still. The dragons' almond green eyes stared hungrily at the new arrivals.

Without diverting his eyes, Louie slowly placed his hand on his dagger. Juggle stood at the front, next to Louie, shielding Tia, Summer and Petra. Squidge tightened her grip around Louie's neck and whispered, "Just wait" in his ear. Louie relaxed his hand.

The dragon on the left of the doorway stretched its neck forward followed by its long tongue. The tongue whipped in and out nearly touching Juggle's chin on the way. Juggle froze. The dragon to the right copied then stepped back. Both dragons lifted themselves onto their hind legs, growing taller and more intimidating. Juggle closed his eyes and gulped with fright.

"Good afternoon, young travellers," said the first dragon in a posh high-pitched voice, "we would like to warmly welcome you to the green lagoon. Please step through."

The six friends stood speechless watching the snarling dragon transform into a posh polite host. Hesitating at first, they slowly stepped off the stone and through the doorway. Still surprised by the voice and demeanour of the dragons, all six continued through with a shocked and unsure look on their faces.

"Please, don't be afraid. We may look like monsters but honestly it's just the exterior. We won't bite I promise," the dragon chuckled.

"Where are we?" Louie asked cautiously finding his feet again.

"You have fallen into the green lagoon. Let me introduce myself and my friend. I am Pip and this is Squeak. We live down here waiting for travellers, such as you. It can get awfully nasty up there when a storm hits." Pip pointed his tail upwards as he spoke.

The second dragon, Squeak, butted in with excitement, "We haven't had visitors for years. No one passes through this area any more. Not since the days of the sisters anyway." Pip nudged Squeak as if to say, be quiet.

"Please," Pip said, "follow me and we will get you dry and cleaned up."

The travellers followed both dragons along a corridor made of seaweed. Starting off dark and gloomy, it gradually became lighter the nearer they got to the next doorway. The dragons Pip and Squeak walked slowly. Petra watched carefully, still unsure of their new acquaintances, and was intrigued when she noticed the skin of the dragons, gradually, change colour from a dirty khaki to a bright white with yellow scales on their back. Pip had slightly more yellow appear than squeak. Petra wondered if this was a sign of age.

Pip placed the spikes of his tail into the centre of the round door, like a key, and when he heard a clunk pushed. The door opened with a creak.

The new visitors were amazed by what their eyes were seeing. The ceiling was transparent showing the bottom of the bog. The room carried on as far as the eye could see, and looking into the distance, Louie noticed a change in the ceiling.

"Why does the ceiling change from brown to clear blue further up that way?" Louie pointed ahead.

"Well," Pip started, "your eyes are good, aren't they? We are standing underneath the bog at this very moment and as you can see it is as dirty as ever. When we are further along the colour becomes lighter because the bog starts to turn into the lake. The bog was put where it is as a deterrent. That is why we had to test your auras with our tongues on your arrival. Luckily none of you are evil. The green lagoon is a double-layered land. Our sky is your land and sits under the whole area of the lake ahead."

Pip walked in front of the group acting as tour guide to his new travelling friends. Squeak was at the back mopping up the muddy footmarks with his tail.

"So you don't have any sky or sun directly above you?" Tia asked confused with the thought.

"Correct. It is always a little embarrassing when nice visitors enter through the back door, seeing a dark and murky tunnel with two monstrous dragons as a welcoming party can be a little intimidating I would imagine, but, even though it's intimidating, it is the only way we can be sure evil doesn't get past the bog and onto the lake. It is so much easier to dispose of any unwanted visitors, by shooting them back up the way they came."

As the tunnel area ended, the space opened up into a bright and airy underground village that bustled with an array of different beings never seen by any of the friends. The ceiling was now clear blue and the sun shimmered through spreading light into the green lagoon. Pip led the group towards a grassy hill not far from the start of a village within the green lagoon. There was a door and two stained-glass windows, imbedded in the front of the hill with pretty flower baskets hanging from each. Pip ushered everyone in through the doorway.

"Take your wet cloaks off here and I will get them dried for you. It shouldn't take long." Pip gathered up the cloaks and handed them to Squeak who took them all back outside and hung them on a tree in the garden.

The house wasn't what you would expect a dragon to live in, much the opposite in fact. The decor was quaint, florally and cosy. Pictures of landscapes hung from the walls not leaving much of the wall itself to be seen. The shelves held trinkets and souvenirs on one side of the room, and china cups and saucers on the other. The house was open plan so the sitting room was shared with the kitchen and dining room. Being only one level the bedrooms were on the same floor towards the back of the house.

"This is beautiful," said Petra, "it's not on our map though." Petra took the map out of her pocket and unfolded it. The map came to life. "Louie, look." Petra grabbed Louie's arm. "The map is adding this land as we stand here." The ink on the page spread, drawing the shape of green lagoon.

"We must be on the right track, P. Why else would it only be showing this?"

Pip, unfazed by the magic page, begun to explain. "This is a map of trust. Onyx was the only witch I knew that could make such a wonderful map of hidden clues. It was made for a purpose and I am guessing you six are that very purpose." Pip held the map and nodded. "Onyx and Mr Pinchbeak were very close friends. She met him when she was hiding from Julique at the very beginning. A very, very wise old owl, if there is anything you need to know he will be the one to help, that's for sure."

"Why's the map just added this land?"

"Onyx was sure that, one day, Julique would try and infiltrate Verlum with the magic of Es'trixia. She travelled to all four corners of Verlum using cloaking spells on lands and items that may hold clues to the scroll. There are a handful of creatures that Onyx trusted with her life including myself and Mr Pinchbeak. We are in a magic circle called the hiders, a group sworn to keep the scroll hidden and protected from Julique.

"Upon contact with a hider you will find the map expands to show your next destination. Even we, as hiders, won't know where you are being led. This was conjured to obviously stop someone who shouldn't have the map continuing. You will find that each time you meet a hider they will test your aura to check that you aren't evil. This will be done in a manner of different ways. You will have to be swift in your task; you don't have much time until the eclipse. The hiders are aware that this adventure has started and of your existence but cannot interfere with your journey. We can only try and keep evil away from your path. If Julique is going to be stopped it has been known that this can only be done by a special group of beings, and you six are that group.

"You must be extra careful now. We've had messages from the woodland folk that a doorway from the underworld has been created already. If this is true Julique has had help from Es'trixia; she would be the only witch powerful enough to break through the protection bubbles surrounding Verlum. Es'trixia would know that a doorway could only be open for a short while, before it sets our alarms off. The locations of the portals are unknown and could be scattered anywhere, so be aware of who you trust. He will unfortunately have spies."

"How did Onyx know all this would happen?" asked Petra.

"When Onyx was in hiding, after the scroll of light and dark was first hidden, her only way of safely contacting the elders' table was through meditation. Thinking deeply about the elders she would connect with them to report her findings of Julique or Es'trixia.

"One day, during her meditation, Onyx was sent images of Julique holding the scroll in the future. On questioning what she was seeing the angels suggested she hid clues across her land providing knowledge of how to stop Es'trixia's evil magic. When Onyx started to do this she realised that she would have to hide clues within clues and spellbind everything that lead to something important." Pip continued to straighten objects on the mantelpiece above the fire. "It was unknown who would be looking for this knowledge in the future. Onyx was in possession of the key to Es'trixia's magic. If Es'trixia found out she would be sure to kill anything that stood in her way to destroy the knowledge. It is still unknown if Onyx managed to hide the knowledge of the key before she went missing."

Squeak handed out sandwiches whilst they waited for their cloaks to dry. Juggle and Tia took the opportunity to wash off the residue of green slime that still held a stench. Squidge, Louie and Summer sat enjoying some proper food whilst Petra continued to quiz Pip about the map.

After handing the sandwiches out to everyone, Squeak went back outside to the tree where their cloaks hung. He stood back and blew out a light breath of fire drying the dripping cloaks instantly, then took them back into the front room and laid them on the table ready for collection.

When everyone had cleaned up, dried off and found their cloak, Pip and Squeak took the group to a doorway.

"This door will take you back up to the surface and put you on the right path for Mr Pinchbeak's island. Remember though, you don't have much time and you still may be a long way from finding your answers. Be safe and good luck."

# Mr Pinchbeak

The door opened and a stepping stone hovered on the other side. The six friends stepped onto the stone and watched Pip and Squeak disappear into the distance as they shot back up to the surface. Being thrown off the stone, and through the air, they all landed on a large lily pad that floated on the surface of the same lake that had once been above them.

Petra looked at the map once again. It now showed the lake's name as Lake Owling. Juggle and Louie used their arms as paddles pushing the lily pad along with the slight current caused by the breeze. The island was within sight but still seemed a fair distance away.

The group felt there had been more obstacles than clues on their journey to find what they were looking for.

"I hope Mr Pinchbeak can help us. So far we've had no clues directing us to any magic," Summer said to Petra and Tia.

"I think this is all part of the plan, Summer," Petra replied. "Maybe we're being led along this path for some particular reason."

"Maybe," Tia agreed.

"Squidge," Tia beckoned, "do you feel strong enough to fly at the moment?"

"Sure. Where do you want me to fly to?"

"Nowhere," Tia replied as she rummaged around in her satchel. "I've an idea that might help us get to the island quicker and it involves both of us." Tia took a piece of old rope from her satchel and tied one end to Squidge's tummy bag and the other end to her own ankle. "If we can use our wings to fly we can pull the lily along quicker. I know neither of us are strong flyers but it's worth a try."

"Great idea, I'll take the middle of the rope." Summer took hold of the rope with both hands as Tia and Squidge flew into the sky in front of the lily pad.

The plan worked well. The lily docked on the island in a small tropical cove with pale sand and palm trees along its banks. The smell in the air was sweet and citrusy. Squidge and Tia landed on the sand and pulled the lily onto the shore of the cove. Louie, Petra, Summer and Juggle jumped out onto the sand; it was warm to touch and felt finer than usual.

Louie looked out onto the lake and admired the clear blue water that only moved when the wind kissed the surface. No other land could be seen from where he stood.

"What does the map say now, P?" asked Juggle.

"We have to follow the sandbank over to the right, then, we should see a pathway towards Mr Pinchbeak's house."

As they walked along the sandbank waves of water started to hit the shore of the lake.

"Hey look at that, out there on the lake," Petra said pointing to the horizon.

All six stood on the sandbank staring at a tornado. The water swirled up into a spiral from the lake.

"I've never known whirlwinds in Verlum," commented Squidge to Summer.

"Neither... have... I," Summer replied, hesitating while she watched.

"Does anyone else think it's getting bigger?" Juggle asked.

Poised in a line they stood staring at the whirling tornado in front of them. It took a moment before Louie realised what was happening.

"That isn't getting bigger, it's getting closer and coming this way. QUICK!" shouted Louie. "RUN."

Louie grabbed Squidge under his arm and followed Juggle, Petra, Tia and Summer into the tall bushes in the opposite direction to the lake. The tornado crept closer; the air rushed frantically around them.

"We have to get underground," Petra shouted.

"How do we do that?" replied Juggle. "We don't have anything to dig with and I can't see any caves!"

Louie, now carrying Squidge on his back again, turned his head to her. "Squidge, my staff, it's in my bag. Can you get it out for me? I might be able to use it to dig." Louie knew this was a stupid idea but he had no others at that moment. If he could get everyone to safety that would be enough, he thought.

Squidge did as Louie asked. Still running in amongst tall bushes, Louie was waiting for the right moment to stop. It wasn't coming. The bushes started to get shorter the further into the island they ran. He could just about see over the top of them now and the tornado was gaining on them quickly; it seemed to be following their exact route through the bushes.

"What do we do? It's getting closer?" Juggle shouted to Louie.

"I don't know." As Louie spoke they entered a clearing with extremely tall trees neatly separated in rows with bushy leaves at the very top.

Petra and Summer ran to the first tree trunk and stopped. They could both see they needed to hold onto something fast before the wind pulled them up into its mouth. Louie, Juggle and Tia followed suit. Holding one another's hands, they circled around the tree and watched the tornado coming straight at them. Louie held Squidge and his staff tightly in front of him. Closing his eyes waiting for the inevitable Louie felt a rush of energy run through his body. Is this what it felt like to be in a tornado? thought Louie.

He opened his eyes to see something amazing happening around him and his friends. The staff was glowing and creating an energy bubble, encapsulating all of them.

Continuing to hold the trunk of the first tree they came too, all looked in amazement at the tornado that was upon them. Standing silently, in the bubble of light, all six were untouched by the whipping wind. Now stood in the centre of the tornado, the circular wall of white wind swirled around them but the centre was silent. Louie and Summer looked up to the top and jumped with fright. An emerald-green eye stared down at them. The eye looked evil and immediately blinked shut when it realised it had been seen, but wasn't shut for long before it opened back up and shone brighter. Suddenly a beam of green light shot out of the eye hitting Louie's bubble with force. The beam bounced off the bubble and hit the inner wall of the tornado several times, eventually striking the green eye. A scream was heard from above followed by a few drops of blood. Louie looked at Summer confused and worried. Time seemed to stand still. Summer tightened her grip on Louie's hand. "What is it?" she whispered.

"It's evil," Louie answered.

"Do you think it's Julique?"

Louie was about to answer Summer but was stopped by a deep, female voice.

"So you think you can defeat me?" the voice boomed from above. "Think again, weak ones. Tell the gods and the angels that they will be answering to Es'trixia soon and they can't stop me." Laughter was heard. "You will never win," the voice said in a patronising manor. It paused for a moment then boomed down again in a rage. "I will kill you all before that ever happens."

Louie felt enraged with anger and scared with the words the voice spoke. He'd never experienced this feeling so intensely before. He lowered his head and tried to control it yet this didn't work. The rage flowed from his head through to his hand that held the staff. Louie concentrated his mind on stopping the voice and that's when everything went silent. The tornado turned from a ripping wind into floating feathers. The eye was gone and no voice could be heard. The bubble also disappeared leaving all six standing around a tree.

Confused with what had just happened Petra was the first to speak. "Louie, your staff, what did you do?"

"I don't know. It just happened. I didn't know the staff was magic!" Louie inspected his staff from top to bottom. "I don't understand. How does it work?"

Petra joined Louie in the inspection. "I don't think it's just the staff Louie... I think you made the staff do what it did."

"Impossible. Surely not?"

"Forget the staff," Juggle panicked, "we should be more worried about the fact an eye spoke to us and said it was going to kill us!" Juggle paced as he spoke.

"Juggle's right." Louie put the staff back in his bag. "The eye was Es'trixia, I'm sure of it. She knew where to look for us and now she's found us. Juggle stop pacing. You're making me more nervous than I already am."

Louie stepped in Juggle's path and placed both hands on his shoulders. "Juggle, we can do this. We have to. We've come too far to turn back. Just think, if we give up we will live under the ruling of Julique and Es'trixia. If we carry on we may still end up living under their ruling, but we can live knowing we tried to stop it."

"Standing here isn't going to get us any closer to it. We need to move fast and find Mr Pinchbeak," Tia interrupted.

"Tia's right let's get back on track," Juggle said in agreement and took a deep breath.

The map was back out in Petra's hands. "It looks as if we're in the right place. To save time I'm going to transform. The trees are so tall we'll never find where we have to be from the ground. I'll fly over the trees and hopefully spot Mr Pinchbeak's home. Everyone wait here."

Tia wasn't sure it was a good idea for Petra to go alone. "Why don't I fly with you, then we will know that you're safe?"

"Sure. We will both fly."

Petra pointed both arms above her head and flapped her arms back down at the same time taking a running jump. As Petra jumped her arms flapped into wings and her body transformed into a beautiful jet-black raven. Petra now flew high into the sky and soared above the treetops. Tia whizzed behind her and they both took a different area zigzagging between the trees hunting for any clues that would lead them to Mr Pinchbeak. Looking down from the sky, Petra admired the tops of the trees. The deep green was beautiful against the blue sky. The trees stood tall on their trunks with bushy leaves that looked like broccoli.

Every tree had a bird house carved into the thick trunks and from the roof of the bird house a wooden sign showed who lived there. Tia spotted Mr Pinchbeak's. The sign was the oldest and tallest of all, sat in the centre of all the trees. She beckoned to Petra pointing at the sign in the distance. Swooping down to the bird house Petra felt uneasy, she held back from landing on the roof and listened.

"What is it?" Tia whispered.

"I'm not sure. Something isn't right. Listen."

Tia listened. "I can't hear anything. It's silent."

"Exactly, the forest is never silent. Something has frightened the life out of this forest. Let's see if Mr Pinchbeak's here."

Both girls quietly landed on the front porch of the bird house and tapped gently on the door. There was no answer, as they tapped again it creaked open. Tia gently pushed the door open fully and whispered, "Mr Pinchbeak, are you in here?" No answer. The two girls cautiously crept in through the front door that led to a sitting room.

Petra looked around the room and pointed to a small table and armchair. Tia went over to it and noticed a cup and saucer next to a teapot and milk jug. The cup was filled with hot tea.

"The tea has just been made, P, it's still hot. Let's look around in case something has happened to him."

They looked around the bird house not finding any clue to where Mr Pinchbeak may have gone in such a rush that he would leave a freshly brewed cup of tea.

"I think we should go back to the others," Tia said.

"So do I but I'm worried about Mr Pinchbeak. Where is he? I'm going to check the bird house next door. Tia you wait here." Tia went to the roof of the house and watched Petra poke her head in through the front door of the house next door. Petra flew back straight away.

"Whoever lived there has left their dinner half eaten. Something has happened. Let's go back to the others."

Just as they were about to fly off a quiet voice was heard. "Pssst? Pssst!"

"Who's that?" Tia turned and looked over her shoulder. "The noise came from over there."

Looking closer at the tree they saw a small barn owl poking its beak over a branch beckoning the two girls with its wing.

"Can you help me?" the little owl whispered, "my foot is stuck. I can't get free."

Tia helped release the little barn owl's foot. "What happened? Why is the forest so quiet?"

The little barn owl rubbed his beak against his foot in an effort to soothe the sprain. "Well it all happened so quickly. One minute I was watering the plants on the roof of my house and the next moment everyone got the warning to move out and fly to safety.

"Unfortunately by the time I realised what was going on, the rush of owls overhead caused me to stumble and that's when my foot got stuck. I have been here ever since, praying whatever scared everything off didn't find me. My name is Halo by the way."

"Hi Halo, I'm Tia and this is Petra. Halo, can you tell us why everyone moved to safety and when this happen?"

Halo sat himself down on the roof to rest his ankle. "All I know is a strong wind kicked up not long before the warning, it felt evil, Mr Pinchbeck was the one that sounded the alarm and that's when everyone flew off, except me obviously."

"Mr Pinchbeak? Where is he now? We really need to see him."

"Everyone flew two forests away. There are some caves hidden just beyond them. I had intended on flying there to let everyone know it was safe to come home. The wind died a death once everyone had flown away, it was very strange. Did you feel it?"

Tia and Petra looked at each other but didn't let on to Halo that they were the reason the evil had arrived on his island in the first place. Both had remembered what Summer had said about not trusting anyone.

Halo stood up and wiggled his ankle checking to see if he was fit enough to fly. "I'll be back soon and hopefully the village will return too." Halo flapped his wings and flew off into the distance.

Petra and Tia returned to the others and explained what had happened. It was decided by the group that they would get closer to Mr Pinchbeak's tree and await his return.

# Time for Tea

The village of Owling returned back to normal and Mr Pinchbeak tested the auras of all six friends by asking them to hold a rock of amethyst one at a time. Once he was satisfied they weren't 'black hearts' they were all allowed up to his home.

"I have been waiting a long time for you to get here," Mr Pinchbeak said opening his stable-style door. The six friends entered one at a time.

Mr Pinchbeak lived in a large tree house, big enough to fit the likes of Juggle and Louie in. Petra was a large-sized bird but Mr Pinchbeak was twice her size and very different than they had expected. He was a very posh spoken, see-through white ghostly figure of an eagle owl.

He settled down on a chair and peered over his half-moon spectacles. As he sat his feathers puffed out, settling slowly. The wind howled through the bird house and swayed with the tree, causing Petra to stumble into a small nest of tables.

"Please sit, Petra," Mr Pinchbeak said in a strict schoolteacher voice, "the rest of you too."

He put his wings out and waved the friends to sit on the floor. "We have a lot to sort out and not much time. If you are here, it means Julique has started to look for the scroll. It is important that you tell me everything that has happened, in precise detail, and exactly what it was that spurred you to look for help." Mr Pinchbeak spoke to the point finishing each word perfectly, accentuating the last letter.

Petra explained what had happened starting with Louie's discovery of awguls in between the Tarania and Verlum border, and their journey to Verlum in search of Onyx's cottage including the spell pool, and the awgul saga at the cottage in Dazlum. Mr Pinchbeak nodded and shook his head in the right places. Once finished she sat and stared at the old owl and couldn't resist asking, "Are you a ghost?"

Slightly more relaxed now the large fluffy owl explained, "I knew Onyx when she first arrived in Verlum after hiding the scroll. She went into hiding straight away from Es'trixia and Julique. One day I was flying over the lake and a wind similar to the one earlier caught me by surprise. My wing became broken by the wind and I fell into the water. I couldn't swim with my broken wing and I started to drown. Onyx was in hiding beneath the lake in the green Lagoon at the time and saw me struggling with my life. Knowing she would never get to me in time to pull me out she placed me in a bubble, but unfortunately half of me had already died leaving my body and soul in two pieces." He took his glasses off and wiped the lenses with an old handkerchief, then placed them back on his beak. "When your body has no soul it has no purpose, so fades away leaving the soul to move on to assist the elders. The transition of my body and soul splitting was interrupted at the point Onyx tried to save me, and amazingly ended up saving my soul and body separately, leaving me with a visual body of a ghost and a soul still attached to this world. From that day on I helped Onyx with anything she needed."

"Was the wind back then exactly the same as today's?" asked Louie.

"Yes. That is why I moved the village out. I did not want anyone to suffer at the evil hands of Julique. The wind is sent from the underworld when Julique is searching for something. Luckily back when Onyx was hiding, the wind missed her because the green lagoon in untraceable. You were all very lucky to survive today." Mr Pinchbeak topped everyone's teacup up and offered around some warm cinnamon buns.

"Mr Pinchbeak," started Summer. "Why have we been led to you?"

He took a sip of his tea and continued, "Onyx needed help during her time in hiding. As she went on her journey, she came across a number of creatures like me that owed her through the help she gave us during a time of need. Her only wish as a gift of thanks was that all of us take an oath to keep the scroll of light and dark safe from evil.

"Onyx knew he would try to resurrect the scroll in the future. She also spoke of a particular group of youngsters being the only ones to stop him. The group, she explained, were special because of the different creations within it, especially the mix of dark and light blood between the gods and angels."

He shuffled again in his chair, rearranging his feathers. "Being holders of light and dark blood, this group would feel the importance of keeping evil from entering the three worlds and becoming an epidemic that it would eventually become. The other hiders and myself were tasked to help the group. I have been waiting a long time for the group to appear and here you all are." Louie and Summer looked at each other surprised at what Mr Pinchbeak was saying.

Mr Pinchbeak rose up out of his chair and stood in the centre of his house. He lifted his wings out to his side spreading each and every feather. His wings began to glow bronze and all the windows and doors slammed shut blocking out any light from outside. Closing his eyes Mr Pinchbeak started chanting in a language none of them understood.

*"Widgika, Sunuika, Tallika Droke. Muuunnuna Unna Yunninun Prone."* The room they all sat in started to spin and oddly without moving them or anything within it, Mr Pinchbeak continued chanting and the spinning became faster and faster. The effect of the spinning made Juggle feel slightly queasy even though the floor stayed still and it seemed that just the

walls turned. With one almighty explosion of light, and the sound of a boom, the house was out of the tree and in the air.

The tree house glided through the air and the walls of it became see-through showing off the world below.

"This… is… amazing," Louie said in awe. He could see Lake Owling as a small blue dot below. They were travelling into the night's sky close to the stars.

"Where are we going?" asked Summer.

"I am to take you to where all the magic started. This should lead you to what it is Onyx wanted you to find."

After some time high in the sky, above the clouds, the house descended and prepared for landing. The walls to the house faded back to their original decor and the windows and door were free of shutters once again. Mr Pinchbeak's bright glow softened before the house landed with a bump. All six got up off the floor and rushed to the closest window. They had landed on a snowy mountain top.

Mr Pinchbeak waddled over to the closet by the front door and rummaged around for a moment until, "Ah ha, here they are." Getting up off his knees he appeared once again in front of the friends holding a number of long coats made of feathers. "You are all to put one of these on. It is bitterly cold outside, and if I am correct, not one of you has ever seen or felt the cold or snow before."

Mr Pinchbeak handed a coat and pair of boots to them one at a time, being sure to give the correct size to the right individual. Amazed at the perfect fit Tia couldn't help but wonder whose feathers they were wearing.

"They were my old feathers," Mr Pinchbeak said, knowing exactly what Tia was thinking. "Before my body perished and knowing the task I had been set, I saved the feathers."

Louie looked at Juggle who was now not stroking the feathers quite as he had upon first being passed the coat.

"It is no different than using feathers that have shed naturally, Juggle," Mr Pinchbeak said, peering over his glasses at Juggle as if to say 'don't be so silly, boy'.

"It is very kind of you to use your feathers in this way," interrupted Squidge feeling the awkwardness of Juggle's actions, "it must have been hard to do this to your own body."

"It was at first but I knew I had to do it for a good reason. Now," he said shuffling over towards the door, "I will be opening the door soon and you will have to be on your way, time is ticking and you are no closer to finding the secret of Es'trixia's magic. When you leave this house you are to head for the next mountain range. You will see it when you step outside and look east. As you look at it from here you will see there are a number of cave entrances on the mountain face. You are to find the Cave of Saphical, it is the third one in as you look left to right from here. Once inside your journey will begin. Do not trust everything you see or hear. It is the cave where magic was born and should only be entered by those with exceptional magic powers. It has been known to trick the most powerful magical beings."

Mr Pinchbeak took a deep breath and slipped back into the role of teacher: he started to speak with a strict and serious tone. "You MUST stay together no matter what. And," he paused once again, "most of all... Remember... This is a cave of both good and evil magic, there is nothing controlling either, they are both raw. You are to find the connection between them both and take it back to Tarania. The scroll can hopefully be found with that knowledge and saved from Julique if you can get to it before he does."

Summer glanced at Louie trying to hide the worry she was feeling. "How will we know when we have found the answer? We don't even know what it looks like!"

"Trust your instinct and you will know," replied Mr Pinchbeak. "Now you must be on your way. When you step outside find the correct route with your map. It should lead you towards the setting sun and try to get to the cave as quickly as you can. The weather can be very erratic and dangerous. I have packed some food and hot honey milk for you all. Now keep warm and good luck – I will be travelling home to Velrum straight away."

"If you're going back to Verlum, Mr Pinchbeak, where are we?" asked Tia.

Mr Pinchbeak waddled to the front door and put his hand on the door handle waiting for them all to fasten their feathered coats and boots before opening it and ushering them out. "You are now in Herbeya."

The door closed abruptly and Mr Pinchbeak was gone. No one said a word.

# The Cold

Louie, Summer, Juggle, Petra, Squidge and Tia stood deep in snow and watched the large bird house hover above the snowy ground before shooting up into the heavy white sky. Within moments the house was out of sight. Standing silent and still the six friends took time to digest everything Mr Pinchbeak had just said, as well as taking in the scenery around them, being hit now and again by the snowflakes that fell intermittently from the sky.

The mountains stood prominent in the distance. The peaks were capped with a glistening of white and blue and the sky changed gradually in gentle waves from red to pink to white. The waves of coloured light were mesmerizing and somehow comforting and warm. Between the mountain top, they were now standing on, and the mountain range they needed to get to, they could just about see a deep valley resting in the middle. Pine trees stood upright in unison with one another, their green coats barely visible underneath the falling snow, and frozen lakes looked like glass floors from a distance. The land was vast. As a first impression Herbeya was impressive and very different to both Verlum and Tarania. Petra was the first to speak. Taking the map out of her satchel she unfolded it and positioned herself so everyone could see.

"Look," she began, "the map has erased our last journey. It now reads 'Herbeya' at the top of the page." Petra pointed at the new title headed at the top of the map. The map now showed mountains and caves.

The route seemed straightforward enough until they looked at it closely and saw there were a few mountains to conquer before arriving at the mountain range intended.

"This is the most exciting day of my life so far," Juggle said dipping his hand into the snow, "I can't believe I am standing in snow. I'd never even imagined what it'd feel like in real life. It's so cold it's refreshing. What do you think, Tia?" Juggle turned to Tia just as she'd made a ball out of the snow and launched it at Juggle. The ball hit Juggle straight on the nose. Tia rolled around the powdery ground laughing hysterically. Juggle, obviously seeing the funny side, was more upset he hadn't got to her first.

"Are you OK, Squidge?" asked Louie concerned she was the smallest one of them all. He turned to Squidge and Summer joined him. Both made sure Squidge was buttoned up tight in her feathered coat and that her boots were on properly.

"I must admit," Squidge said shivering and lifting her foot up for Summer, "I initially thought my fur would be enough to keep me warm. I couldn't have been more wrong."

Petra stood on her own gazing at the map. "Herbeya," she muttered to herself in disbelief, "I can't believe it." The map showed the mountains they had to reach then stopped as it had done at the green lagoon. Petra had dreamt of visiting Herbeya. It was probably the best world for any healing witch to live or visit.

The elders had given Herbeya a natural cure for every ailment you could possibly imagine. Little was really known about the land itself by Petra's family; she had only ever heard tales that had been passed down through the generations from her great-great grandmother who'd once visited. Back in those times all three lands were open for all to come and go as they pleased. It wasn't until Julique turned 'rogue angel' that the lands were on lockdown and permission from the elders was needed for anyone to enter or leave. Petra clearly remembered the tales. They involved potions that were now rare because the ingredients could only be found in Herbeya, and the constant shift in weather on the land had been a danger point when visitors would visit the land unprepared.

The wind around the six friends began to pick up encouraging the snow to fall heavier.

"The weather's turning. We should start moving," Petra suggested, "and follow the map as best we can whilst trying to keep safe and sheltered. Look," Petra pointed at the map again, "this path is along the side of a mountain edge. If we stay on that path we should stay out of the snowfall. I remember being told stories of the snowstorms and from what I recall they are quite horrific, deadly in fact."

The friends set off moving awkwardly through the snowy ground, along the ridge of the mountain top Mr Pinchbeak had dropped them off on. They headed for the closest sign of a track that would lead down to the valley in the distance. Each hoped the journey would be easier than it looked but, in the same breath, knew there would be no chance of any such luck.

# Talented Angel

Julique was recruited by the elders' table during his last years in school as a senior student. He was famous for his knowledge of beings and creations born at the elders' table. With the knowledge and interest he held, he became invaluable to the ingredients of new creations and the improvement of beings of all kinds. This was to no detriment to the early creations of the elders but they found that some early creations weren't as strong and died early in life.

Julique was from a well-known family of angels. They'd all had the honour of working with the elders at some point. His father was a professor of the sciences and his mother was an artist. The combination was perfect, one would assist in the making of creations (new creatures) whilst the other would sketch the 'would be' appearance. The family were as you would expect, very loving and lived to help creation become great and peaceful.

After being trained by all that sat at the table Julique soon became the expert on successful mixes of creation. The success was determined by the level of happiness and goodness they spread – it was the aim of the elders to create one world that would house a mixture of creations to live peacefully and happily in and assisting those creations that were not so lucky in their existence and hopefully this would keep evil at bay.

As the years moved on Julique became reluctant to make all creations as good and as kind as the elders had wished. He felt that the world would drown in its own happiness and become complaisant about the happiness they had and in time expect the happiness without earning it. Julique strongly believed that happiness should be earned rather than given upon birth and the more 'good will' achieved through helping others the happier their lives should be, but he also believed that not all creations should be as good as others. This to Julique was becoming boring as well as making his job redundant. Soon the creations would be finished and this was going to happen fast if everything created was good. From a young age, Julique had set his sights on becoming the most powerful elder in existence.

The elders weren't aware of his feelings to start with. They trusted all he suggested, but after a time the elders got word that some creations were acting in ways towards others that were not nice at all.

What Julique hadn't thought about was the fact that you would need to guide those that wouldn't naturally feel they had to do good in the world and once the seed of evil had been sewn it wouldn't be easy to undo.

The whole process that had worked for thousands of years began to fail because of Julique and his foresight into how the world should be. The whole point of the elders' table was so no single creation was created on one elder's say so; it was the thoughts and feelings of all that made what they do work, thus not making any one elder more powerful than the rest.

When Julique fell from the grasps of the elders his mother and father disappeared in shame and haven't been seen since. It's thought they were probably dead now anyway but were so ashamed at their son's actions they wouldn't be welcome at the table ever again. It was at this point Julique's plan to destroy the scroll of light and dark began.

# Light and Dark Blood

The elders were at creation 6,394,558,661 and in the middle of creating a small red insect with black spots on its wings when the news arrived at the table of the astonishing love binding between a light blood angel called Alauria and a dark blood God called Thelor.

The news was unheard of. The two bloods had never mixed by way of love before and it was thought to have been impossible. Everyone at the table rejoiced at the news and the possibilities that now stood before them. This could solve the solution of evil with the power of this combination.

Angels and gods worked well together in keeping the peace in their lands. They had always lived very different lives but kept a strong bond between themselves. They were the higher beings of creation and eventually would fade into the background once the elders had completed their work at the table, leaving the beings of the lands to guide themselves without the continuous help of angels or gods.

The differences between both bloods is extreme. Dark blood is that of strong beings that have the powers of all elements, giving them the strength and will to fight anything that stands in the way of keeping the 'great of good' flowing, including one another which had been known from time to time. Angels on the other hand, having light blood, are the makers of peace and hope and solved problems by providing positivity and the healing hand. They would use guidance instead of force to get results. The blood of both, when put together, naturally repelled like two magnets shown to each other, believed to be the natural sign that the two were not meant to be as one even though they both strove for the same result.

Thelor and Alauria were the first of their kind to break the natural rules of the two bloods. They first met whilst assisting the fairy folk in Laudres Forest. The toadstool breeding programme had grown out of control and they were tasked, as students, to calm the growth by any means possible. As time passed the issues of their differing opinions on how to control the toadstools became a fun challenge for both of them. Their friendship grew and eventually turned into love. Both learned to respect each other's differing ways and after many attempts at solving the problem it became apparent that, combining both of their strengths and powers together, the results were astounding and problem solved.

Thelor proposed to Alauria with the blessing of both families.

Once married it wasn't long until Alauria gave birth to three beautiful girls. The babies were much anticipated by the elders as they would be a true mix of light and dark.

Of course Julique was enraged with anger and came up with his plan to get close to the scroll by becoming an elder. Of course the evil engulfed him as he became obsessed with the thought of controlling the table and evil set into his soul, causing him to commit the unthinkable crime of murder.

One night during the half-moon ceremony, held below the elders' table, Julique broke into the tomb, where the scroll of light and dark was held expecting to steal the scroll from under the elders' noses, but unbeknown to him, the scroll was guarded at all times by three senior elders. Confronted by the three elders who wanted an explanation as to why he was in the tomb, Julique, not taking kindly to being questioned, grabbed the dagger kept behind his wings and slit the throats of all three. As a statement of his anger Julique lined them up against the trunk to which the scroll was secured. Leaving the tomb he decided that it was time to destroy the so-called family of light and dark.

Julique headed to where Thelor lived and planted the dagger amongst his tools. It wasn't long before the alarm was sounded and the bodies of the dead angels were discovered. Julique quickly made it back to the table in enough time to suggest that he had seen someone of similar appearance to Thelor leaving the tomb with a dagger in his hand. No matter how much Thelor persisted with his innocence, there was still the fact the dagger had been found in his tools by the guardians of the elders. By this along with Julique's word, he was doomed.

Framing Thelor for the murders he was banished to the underworld immediately and separated from Alauria and his daughters forever. Julique had the elders believing that this was the outcome of light and dark bloods mixing.

Of course, as always with evil, it can only hide itself for so long before it starts to seep out of the eyes and become visible to all. In time others at the table started to see the power-hungry changes in Julique. It wasn't until the daughters of Thelor and Alauria were older that his true evil became uncontrollable and the truth of what he had done was discovered.

# Es'trixia

Slamming his fist on to the arm of his chair, Julique stood up and shouted at the top of his voice:

"You have failed me on a simple task, you cretins. I think it's time for you all to be dismissed for eternity!" Julique shot a bolt of fiery ice at the leader of the awguls. On hitting the awgul his body turned to ice and exploded. Julique didn't stop until the entire group of awguls were dead and in pieces on the floor in front of him.

"Belf?" screamed Julique at the top of his voice, "get here now." Belf was never far away from his master; he'd seen others perish for failing to be quick upon his beckon. Belf entered through the archway and bowed his head, answering to his master's call.

"Get this cleaned up, I cannot bear to see or smell this mess for another moment." Julique turned his back to Belf and started pacing in deep thought. How was he going to find the key to where the scroll was hidden? Who could he use to do the job without messing it up? Could he complete this before it was too late? The answers were just not coming to him. He needed to think clearly but there was no time for this. The situation was becoming urgent. A green haze caught his eye entering through the arch.

"Es'trixia," he said firmly without lifting his eyes from the ground he was pacing. "What is it now?"

Es'trixia did not appreciate the spiteful tone of his voice towards her and this raised the hackles on her back. Forcefully she flew into the room towards him and picked him up by his throat. She threw him against the nasty uneven wall of sharp, jagged rocks.

"Don't you dare use that tone with me, you filthy creature." As she spoke her face morphed from a very pretty feminine look to the face of a demon. Baring her sharp teeth only a sliver away from Julique's cheek, she bore her eyes into his and hissed with anger spitting acid from her mouth. "Show me some respect."

Julique shook with terror inside but tried to hide it from her.

The witch morphed back into a beautiful woman and lowered Julique's feet back onto the ground. He slumped onto the floor, his wings damaged having been pushed against the razor-sharp rocks on the wall.

"Oh dear, dear, Julique, what have I done? I don't know what came over me." Es'trixia liked to play the 'good witch, bad witch' routine. She thought it reminded Julique just who was in control, and of course she was more powerful than him. Yet she needed him to keep her hidden under his elders' cloak until she had the scroll. "Look what you have done to yourself. Your wings are bleeding."

"Get off me," Julique said through gritted teeth. He pushed her hands away from his shoulders. He knew full well what she was playing at. "I am no fool, Es'trixia, your games are pathetic."

"Pathetic they might be, Julique, but remember, you need me." She smiled and poured herself a drink, "Would you like one?" With no answer from Julique she poured one any way and left it on the table for him to collect when he'd sorted himself out.

"I had an interesting run in with some young beings whilst I was out hunting," she continued, settling herself down on Julique's throne, knowing this would annoy the hell out of him. "They, it seems, have been looking for the scroll." She took a long sip of her drink, then swirled the ice in the glass with her long fingernail waiting for a response. "They were an interesting group, very young and probably one day quite powerful, but not yet. I gave them a taste of my magic which should be enough to panic them for a while."

"Where were they?" The response was short and to the point.

"Verlum." she replied. "Lake Owling to be exact. It came to my attention that they had been to the cottage once lived in by Onyx. I have spies out there who will do anything to keep their families from being, how shall I put it?" she giggled childishly, "killed." Taking a further sip from her drink, she continued, "They had help from the elders' table too, a scruffin."

"Impossible," Julique scoffed. "The elders cannot interfere with creations and therefore cannot send helpers down to assist individuals." Julique was now standing again. He ignored the glass poured by the witch and instead held the decanter of drink and drank directly from it to ease the pain in his wings.

"Are you calling my sources liars, Julique?" Es'trixia asked with an evil tone, lifting only her eyes from her glass, still stirring with her long fingernail.

"Not liars, Es'trixia, just misunderstood." He hated being cautious about what he should and shouldn't say; it made him feel weak. "How did you know they were looking for the scroll?"

"One of the young ones had been sent from the gods and the other sent from the angels. I am aware that Onyx set about scattering clues around all the lands ready for someone to find when things became desperate. The keepers of the clues are starting to surface and we just need one of them to slip up and maybe come out of the woodwork sooner than they need to. If we can track these young ones it may lead us to where we want to go without the hard work."

"Where are they now?"

"That is for you to sort out. You need to send your minions to the last place I saw them and track them from there. Oh dear, you can't, you've just killed them, you idiot!"

"I have others I can send Es'trixia and my work force is not your business."

Es'trixia smirked once again knowing the buttons to push for a reaction. "Point taken, Julique." She would let him have that one, she thought, calmly taking another sip from her glass. "Ideally the group need to be stopped in their tracks. If they can't get to the clues they can't get to the scroll which leaves us to find the scroll without their interference."

Julique pushed his anger back inside himself and refrained from losing control. "Why can you not seek them out through your third eye? Would that not be quicker than tracking?"

Rising up from the throne Es'trixia slowly glided towards Julique as she thought out loud. "The young god has something with him that detected my third eye. He has the gods' staff of gold." She paused and thought for a moment as if recollecting memories. "I thought I had destroyed all of them but obviously not. Now the staff has been activated and knows of my existence, I cannot detect anything within its range. It will protect its master until his death, but interestingly the young god seemed shocked when the staff used its magic. My guess is he doesn't know its capabilities." She stopped in front of Julique and stared into his eyes. "Are we friends again, my dear Julique?" She placed her hand on his cheek and stroked it with her thumb. "Let's not fall out again, I just hate for you to see that wicked side of me." Es'trixia smirked once again, knowing that Julique couldn't bear to look at her, let alone pretend to believe the lies she was speaking, but he went along with it.

He stopped himself from shuddering at her disgusting evil touch; he wanted to pull away but knew if he did she wouldn't take kindly to it. He'd already learnt not to push her too far. She had proved that she was far stronger.

"It's forgotten," he managed to say. "We are both under pressure to achieve the same result, that's all, I am sure there won't be a repeat of that behaviour by either of us."

Lowering her hand she nodded in agreement and walked towards the arched entrance. "Keep me informed of your minions' progress. I will give you the exact whereabouts they were last seen when you have found your minions capable. We have no time for screw-ups. The eclipse will soon be upon us and we must have the scroll in our hands or it will be too late."

"Leave it with me."

Es'trixia left the cave leaving Julique poised on his throne thinking of who to use for the next part of the plan.

"Come on think," he said to himself out loud, "I am not going to give that witch the pleasure of mocking me again. I need a creature that can fit in away from the underworld that has some brain power." Upon that Julique bellowed to Belf, who scurried in within moments and stood with his head bowed once again.

"Belf, go below to the firepit and get me the master of the sluths. It is urgent so don't keep me waiting." Julique dismissed him with a wave of his hand and Belf disappeared on the spot.

A sluth is a snake-like creature, even though they mainly moved by slithering along the ground they also had the ability to grow arms and legs at any given time, allowing them to stand alongside other creatures. They were smarmy and deceitful creatures, making them perfect for the job, but unlike the awguls they had a brain and knew how to use it.

The master of the sluths appeared within moments of Belf being sent to the firepit to get him.

"You summoned me, sire?" the sluth said as he changed from a snake to a standing creature.

"Yes, I did."

# The Hike

Thick solid clear blue icicles hung from everything they passed. They all felt they had travelled miles when in fact it was not very far at all. The falling snow covered any previous footpaths that once existed, making the journey slower.

The map Petra held now showed their route zigzagging across Herbeya to the cave of Saphical. This was the safest and easiest route rather than climbing up and down mountains and sliding over lakes that were in their way. The map would keep them from potentially dangerous routes.

They all sat and caught their breath after the hike down the first mountain.

Louie perched on a fallen snow-covered tree. "I think we are doing well considering none of us have ever stepped on snow before. It's certainly not easy stuff to walk on, especially when it is nearly up to your knees."

"I'm not sure about that," Petra replied holding the map out in front of him. "Look," she pointed to where they were and where they had to get to, "we have hardly moved." Petra slumped down next to Louie, tired and slightly disheartened.

Louie, for the first time during this journey, had a moment of doubt about accomplishing the task he'd offered to fulfil. Petra was never down hearted and this worried Louie more than anything. He took the map from Petra's grip as she put her head in her hands. He looked at his friends standing in front of him and realised he couldn't let them see or feel his defeat at this stage of the journey.

"OK. So we have quite a way to go, and preferably before nightfall, but we can do this. Look," Louie stood again to show keenness, "the map is showing a route that looks flat and sensible. All we have to do is follow this at a quick pace and I reckon we can get there before the moon is at its highest. Is everyone OK to carry on?"

Juggle was shivering every now and again. "I think we should have some more of the hot honey milk that's in our food bags, just to keep us going until we can stop again. Also I have got to stretch my wings. Although they have been crumpled I am getting cramp with this coat restricting them."

Tia giggled at Juggle being dramatic. "You'd better be quick with stretching them, in these temperatures they are likely to freeze. Don't forget your delicate little wings have never been subjected to such harsh conditions." Tia pulled a baby face as she spoke.

"How very sympathetic of you, Tia. If I didn't know you better I would have thought you were being kind! Your wings aren't as big as mine so stop thinking I'm being dramatic. I had a very bad fall on these beauties and I think I was very brave considering the pain."

Juggle and Tia smiled at each other knowing they were both joking.

Squidge, Summer and Louie helped one another pour the honey milk out of the hot flasks. Once they had finished their quick warming drink break they packed up their tankards and got on the path shown by the map.

It was dusk by the time they had reached the other side of the frozen lake, which on the map looked as if they had travelled well over halfway. The friends followed the sweeping path around the lake towards two cliff faces that stood prominent; the path naturally led into a canyon between the cliff faces. Unlike the previous path the ice did not reflect the natural light as it had during sundown, the canyon was dark and ghostly. Not being able to see anything ahead Summer got a glass ball out of her bag. She said a few words and the ball lit up and floated a few steps ahead of them all.

"The ball will not last forever but it will see us past this area at least," she said.

Louie thought it was only right that he lead the way ahead. He looked up at the cliff faces he was walking between: they were jagged and vicious, slanting at an angle over the path they were on. The icy ground made the whole experience more spooky with the creaking sound it made as their feet moved over what was once water. Louie shivered at the thought of the cliffs crumbling down on top of him, let alone the ice beneath his feet cracking. The two separate cliff faces practically touched each other at the top.

"Be really careful not to crack the ice! The water under the ice would kill us if we fell in," Louie whispered. Everyone in turn began to place their feet carefully as they walked.

Squidge stayed by Louie's side holding onto the sleeve of his feathered coat. "I keep thinking I'm seeing figures in the cliff face, Louie," Squidge said slowly and quietly.

"It's quite a scary path, Squidge," Louie whispered back, "but I think it's your mind playing tricks with the shadows in the ice." Louie looked about quickly hoping not to see anything.

The crunching of the icy snow under his feet became louder as the two cliff faces above him started to join, creating an extremely tall tunnel. The once white icy walls were now a dark colour. Icicles as tall as Louie hung from the most slanted parts of the cliff face. The path ahead was unknown and this meant danger. There was no way of telling how far they had to go and no landmarks to assist in telling them how far they had gone. The eerie feel was accentuated by the coldness and silent sound of snow falling above them.

Their footsteps began to echo until Louie and Squidge stopped suddenly and listened. Both turned to each other in a panic of what they couldn't hear. There was no one behind them, they were gone. Louie picked Squidge up and threw her on his back. His body turned stone cold with fright; something felt wrong in the pit of his stomach.

"Squidge. Where have they gone? How could we lose them? They were right behind us." He began running, as well as he could, back along the track he'd just been on, but the ball of light was fading and it was too slow to keep up with Louie's speed. The sound of the ground cracked in unison with the movement of Louie's feet.

"We don't even know when we lost them and soon we won't even have any light to help find their tracks. Squidge you look along the cliff faces and I will look on the ground, there must be some clue as to where they have disappeared."

The ball of light had near on faded into darkness now and Louie was beginning to slow down as the cold air stole his breath.

The bitter wind picked up using the canyon path as a wind tunnel. Louie stopped and stood on the spot not moving. Squidge tightened her arms around Louie's neck.

"Whatever happens, Squidge, do not let go of me."

Louie racked his brain for an idea of what to do next, though without light everything seemed impossible. He started to move his back and Squidge closer to the cliff face. "Glow-worm," he whispered loudly. Reaching into his satchel Louie pulled out a jar with his little glow-worm in. "It's better than nothing, Squidge. If I hold it out in front with my staff it will give us time to search a little bit further along the path. They couldn't have just disappeared: they have to be around here somewhere."

Louie hooked the jar to the end of his staff and pointed it out in front of them. The wind had died again.

Standing still at first, allowing their eyes to adjust, Squidge suddenly put her hand over Louie's mouth.

"Louie I can hear something."

Louie listened and Squidge was right, there was a noise not far from where they were standing and seemed to be moving in their direction. "It sounds like something is sliding along the floor."

Louie anxiously lifted his staff slightly higher and further forward knowing that he was going to have to see what was with them.

Within a split second of raising the staff Squidge uttered five words in Louie's ear, "Run now. It's a sluth."

Louie without hesitating, dropped the jar off the end of his staff, turned back towards the old route and ran as quick as possible.

"Just keep running, Louie. If it catches us we will be killed. He has been sent from the underworld."

With that explanation Louie tried to pick up more speed but the icy snow beneath his feet was against him. His feet slipped with every step he was taking.

"We have nowhere to hide, Squidge, and I don't know how long I can run like this for. The ice is slowing me down."

Squidge looked back and could sense the sluth gaining on them.

"How are you at climbing?" Squidge asked. "It might be our only chance of losing it. If we can get even our height off the ground we may confuse it enough to carry along the path."

Louie knew he only had one chance of getting this right and if he missed his footing or grip on the cliff face at any point they would be dead for sure.

Louie was a good athlete and though his strongest sport was running and throwing he also excelled at jumping, Louie quickly recalled his lessons and went for it.

"Hold on, Squidge."

Louie stopped, mid pace, and jumped at speed towards the cliff face hoping with all his heart that his hands would find something to grip onto. Grabbing whatever he could Louie dug his fingers into the ice and held on with his life.

His fingers were no longer a part of him; they had frozen and he now had no control over them. He felt himself falling back towards the ground. His fingertips latched onto a thin ledge. As one hand grabbed it the other followed quickly and then his feet on a lower notch. He knew that he would have to try and climb higher to be out of reach and undetectable. He quietly fumbled his feet onto a higher notch followed by his hands, desperately trying not to push any loose snow onto the ground below as he did so.

"Stop," Squidge whispered. "Stay still."

The sound of something sliding along the ice beneath them became louder then suddenly stopped. The darkness seemed to magnify any sound. Louie tried to stop breathing as it seemed so loud in his head.

A sporadic hissing sound interrupted the silence along with the movement of the sluth below, then silence again. Louie could feel his hands slipping on the icy ledge. He tried to squeeze it harder in the hope his hands would stick, but it didn't help. One hand started to slip then so did the other. He could feel his weight falling back as his grip loosened.

"Louie, if we slip we die," Squidge whispered.

"I can't control it." With those words, both hands were now detached from the cliff face and he was falling.

Before either of them could prepare, Louie's body hit the ground. He scrambled to his feet, losing grip with Squidge still wrapped around his neck. Without warning something whipped his shins knocking him back onto the solid ice floor. His shins stung with the blow.

There was nothing he could do. the snake-like creature was now towering over them. Louie quickly pushed his back up against the cliff face hoping to balance himself and use his staff to fend off the vile creature.

The sluth moved closer. Louie could feel its tongue tasting the air he was breathing. All of a sudden the creature seemed to pull away and made a loud hissing sound.

Squidge tightened her arms and buried her head in Louie's neck knowing that this was the end of them both. They were going to die. Louie turned his head towards Squidge realising what was about to happen. "Sorry, Squidge," Louie said, at the same time the words left his mouth he felt hands gripping his arms and legs.

The hands started to pull him into the cliff face. He felt colder than before. Had he died? he wondered. Was this how you felt? Maybe he had died a while ago but due to the darkness hadn't realized. Louie's mind raced. He couldn't move, his body was frozen. What about Squidge more importantly. Had he left her behind because he had been too weak to fight like a true god? His heart sunk at the thought of little Squidge being alone in the dark with a vile creature on the prowl. The hands continued to pull him backwards and his body became slightly warmer allowing some feeling to return. His first thought was to check if he still had a little pair of paws gripped around his neck.

"Squidge, please still be with me?" he managed to gasp whilst his teeth chattered uncontrollably.

"I'm here, Louie. What's happening to us?"

"I don't know but keep hold of me." Louie realised it was becoming easier to move his head. He managed to glance down at the hands on his legs; they were large, grey and hairy with long claws at the end of the fingers. The arms weren't completely visible but seemed thicker compared with his own.

In the same moment the warmth returned to his body, he was forced backwards falling once again to the ground. "Ouch," muttered Louie. He sat up slowly taking in his surroundings.

He had just fallen out of a wall of ice.

"We have been pulled through a wall of ice," Squidge said in amazement. Finally, she let go of Louie's neck and sat up next to him.

"By who?" Both turned away from the wall and were met by a group of very large, grey furry creatures standing behind them in a sort of corridor.

Not knowing whether these creatures were friend or foe Louie grabbed Squidge and pulled her in close.

The largest of the grey creatures stood in the centre of the others and let out an almighty roar baring his long sharp teeth and snarling as he finished. The other creatures joined in the snarling. It was then that Louie actually considered pushing himself back through the wall of ice. 'Would it have been easier to fight one sluth than a group of snarling teeth baring creatures?' Louie thought.

At that moment three of the creatures pounced straight towards Louie and Squidge. They jumped into the wall. The claws of one of the paws dusted the top of Louie's head luckily with no damage at all. By the time Louie had checked to see if his scalp was still intact the creatures had disappeared back into the ice wall. All that could be seen from where Louie and Squidge sat was the blurred sight of red liquid splattering against the other side of the wall. Then it stopped.

A long thin shadow was seen to be thrown against the same wall of ice sliding down until slumped on the ground.

Louie turned his back against the horrific scene to be met by the largest of the grey furry creatures walking with purpose towards him. His stomach turned with nerves, he felt himself wince. The creature took hold of Louie and Squidge by the scruff of their necks and hoisted them up off the ground. Squidge whimpered slightly as the creature grabbed her neck fur, catching her skin at the same time.

"Watch it," Louie shouted, "you're hurting her!"

The creature growled and continued along the edge of the ice walled tunnel with his catch in hand.

It was a nasty sight back out on the other side of the iced wall. The once white snow was now a bright shade of red. Not far from where Louie and Squidge had held on to the cliff edge for dear life, now lay one half of a dead snake-like body once belonging to a sluth.

It was still pitch black on the cold side of the wall but it was easy to make out the two halves of the sluth being slung over the shoulder of the creatures that seemed to glow in the dark.

The creatures did not waste a kill. This would be the starter on their evening menu.

The ice tunnel seemed never ending. Louie got used to the creature's hands around his neck and, in a bizarre way, hoped they wouldn't actually get to the unknown destination. The creature ducked down on entering a new room. The room they were now entering was very different from the environment they had just been in. It was welcoming. With the calm pastel tones to the ice-built room Louie could smell lavender and felt unusual warmth radiating from the walls around him.

The walls were opaque throughout making it a bit easier to guess what they were going to be faced with next. In the room opposite Louie could make out a couple of smaller figures. The creature moved through the archway to the centre of the room and dropped Louie and Squidge on the spot. Before they hit the floor the creature had turned around and bolted back through the arch, on all fours, and out the room.

Squidge tried to stand up from the heap she had just been dropped in whilst rubbing her neck. Louie stayed in his dumped position and slowly looked around the room.

"The room is almost beautiful," Squidge whispered, "it is very calming and smells so relaxing. What do you think it's used for? Are they trying to trick us?"

"I really don't know yet. We need to figure out if we have been rescued or captured and at the moment I am no closer to guessing which."

Squidge tiptoed closer to the wall where she could see the figures in the next room and tried to listen in for clues.

"Who do you think is in there?" Squidge put her ear up to the wall hoping they wouldn't be able to see her shadow because she was white and small. "I'd say there are about five different voices in there. One is certainly taking the lead though."

Louie now standing, wandered around the room: though very plain with bits and bobs nowhere to be seen, it had the most beautiful ice carvings Louie had ever seen, not that he had seen any before, but the intricate detail was astounding.

Louie beckoned Squidge over to where he was standing. They both stood back from the wall and realised that the circular room had a story carved in its walls all the way around. The reflection of the pastel colours within the room hit the carvings, which made them look as if they were moving.

Starting from the right-hand side of the entrance the pictures showed three young girls with two adults looking up at the stars and one of the stars shining down upon them. The next was of three angels all holding a scroll of parchment between them. As the pictures continued around the room they told the story of the scroll of light and dark. The story matched that of the one told by Louie's father, including the murder of the elders by Julique.

"Footsteps," Louie whispered loudly in panic, "quick stand over here."

They both moved opposite the entrance and watched the wall melt away followed by the entry of another furry creature.

Louie and Squidge stared, intently, at the creature. Its head morphed from a grizzly teeth-baring, overly furry faced beast, to a much less intimidating, softer look, with teeth no longer being the main feature noticed at first glance.

As its height shrunk it developed a limp in one of its legs. The transformation concluded with a long, blue, hooded cloak appearing from the furry neck growing downwards until it dragged along the floor behind. The creature stopped in the centre of the room allowing the cloak to settle in a semi-circle behind.

Taking a walking stick out from beneath his cloak the creature used it to assist with balance whilst he stood still in front of his guests.

"Welcome," the creature said, "you are wondering what I am, are you not?"

Louie and Squidge stayed quiet.

"My name is Snow and I am a furgan. I am the oracle of the furgan tribe. We are creatures of the ice worlds here in Herbeya and are born to protect all that is good and stop all that tries to harm Herbeya or our people in it. Unfortunately, for them, we tend to permanently stop those creatures that are evil. Although none of their bodies go to waste, we do eat them."

Squidge pulled a sour face; the thought of eating another being made her feel queasy.

"I'm Louie and this is Squidge. I don't suppose you know where our friends are? We lost them just before we were attacked by a sluth."

"We were watching you from the moment you entered the ice valley and fortunately for your friends we managed to intervene before the sluth realised they were there. Your friends are safe, in fact they are probably close to planning what to do next on your journey to save our worlds from evil."

"Can we see them? We don't have time to detour from our journey. We have to get to the caves in the mountains opposite this valley."

"Yes I am aware of where you need to go, but first you must understand what may be waiting for you in those caves. The sluths have been sent from the underworld, meaning Julique knows your whereabouts. If he is sending sluths it is a sign he is now panicking and desperately needs to stop you. The sluths are probably the most reliable of underworld creatures to carry out tasks without messing them up. He is showing his hand sooner than I thought he would. It won't be long before he realises he needs to send more to stop you."

Louie felt confused and now worried for, not his safety, but the safety of his friends. This was no longer a journey of adventure it was a death sentence. If things went wrong, and the possibility of that happening was becoming increasingly high after the recent events, it would be his entire fault.

Snow watched Louie as the colour drained from his face.

"Louie. You must not doubt yourself as a leader. You must also not underestimate the courage and strength of your friends. You were all put together for a reason. Fate has played a big part in this plan so trust in the journey you have been put upon. I will take you to your friends if you promise to erase the failing thoughts from your mind. The thought of failure itself is enough to start the spiralling path of failure, of which you will have no control over once it gets started."

Squidge took hold of Louie's hand and gave it a reassuring squeeze.

"Now," Snow continued, "if you are ready to continue I will be happy to take you to your friends."

Snow turned to the wall that Squidge had been listening up against. He took a few steps towards the wall and placed the end of his walking stick up to a small triangular shape that sat as a randomly carved symbol. An archway opened into a side room and there, sitting around a table, were his friends and now for certain adventure companions.

"Squidge," Summer breathed with relief as she ran over to her very much adored little friend, "I missed you and was so worried I would lose you." Summer took Squidge into her arms and gave her the biggest cuddle ever, kissing her head all over then finished by just holding her tight.

Louie didn't quite get the same sort of welcoming party. Petra was sitting with her head in a book with Tia both looking very busy.

"It's about time you got here," Petra started.

Of course, really, she was worried out of her mind but she trusted the creatures that had taken them in to save them all. Juggle on the other hand did stride over and grab Louie's shoulders.

"What in the name of Tarania happened to you two?" Juggle gave Louie a manly awkward hug then put him down quickly.

"What happened to us? More to the point, what happened to you lot? You were there one moment then gone the next and not even a sound to warn us!"

"We didn't have the opportunity to warn you. Before we even knew what was happening we had been pulled through the ice wall by the furgans. It wasn't until we were through the wall we realised why they had done what they had. A creature was following us all but luckily hadn't quite caught up close enough to see how many of us there were, so you were the prey. Not ideal but we are all safe now."

"Not ideal? You're not wrong there! We thought we were dead," Louie said in disbelief. Turning back to Snow Louie asked, "What are these sluth creatures, Snow?"

"Sluths are born into the underworld. They have a snake's body but can transform by growing arms and legs to fit in with our worlds. The sluths are one of the more intelligent creatures from the underworld hence Julique's move to send them after you. It's unusual for them to fail their tasks and for that reason it was necessary for us to completely dispose of the body. Sluth wouldn't be a first choice for lunch; they tend to be a little tough to chew!

"If we hadn't have acted quickly, you would most certainly be dead. As a group you all need to understand the danger you face. You are all blessed with one another's friendship, and you all have your own place within the group, but it is more important now than ever that you each use your individual skills and bring them together when needed. Julique will find it challenging to break through the barrier of goodness that protects you all because your friendship is so strong."

Snow walked over to the table the friends were sat around. "Now the cave that you are to travel to next," he continued, "is where your journey really begins. Caves are dangerous places: they are the mouths to the underworld. Things change rapidly in caves. All caves have at least one portal that leads into the underworld. The creatures and Julique are not aware of all the portals in our world. They were placed there by the elders when the underworld was first created so the elders could enter at any time. We have traced most of them and put up extra protection to stop evil from entering, but, if Es'trixia has been involved she has probably tried to trace the portals to counteract the spells we have cast upon them.

"Louie, Snow turned to Louie and pointed at his satchel, "you have a staff from the gods. Is that right?"

"Yes." Louie slid the staff out of the top of his very wet satchel that now sat at his feet under the table.

"You are to take note of the staff. When it is unsure of the energy around you it will change in its appearance. This is its way of warning you. The warning will never be the same and it will be subtle. It may be a slight change in colour or even a force field around you, but you will know. You and the staff will eventually be in tune as one. It's at that point you will not have to watch the staff for changes. You will feel it. But be aware. Es'trixia, we thought, successfully banished all staffs owned by the gods. When she realises you have one she will make it her mission to take it from you. They hold great power even in the wrong hands."

Louie placed the staff on the table in front of the group, now feeling slightly weary of touching it.

Snow continued, "The staff was made to protect gods from evil energies and being uncontrollably used by evil. By giving signs that evil is close it allowed the gods time to react. Do not underestimate the strength of the staff. It will protect you but also feed from your emotions, so bear this in mind. The staff will not stop just because a friend or loved one is in the way. It has been attached to you now so you alone are what it will protect. You are its priority."

Louie picked the staff back up and stared at it in his hand with a different vision than before. Little did he know that this was such a powerful tool. His father had not said anything about the staff. No warnings. Nothing! What was he thinking, giving his 'inexperienced son such a powerful tool?

"You must shut off the doubt you are feeling Louie." Snow raised his voice in frustration whilst hitting his walking stick on the floor beside him and shaking his head.

"You have to realise that these emotions are a feeding ground for anything with evil blood. They will sense these feelings before you even realise that you are feeling them yourself. Don't let that be the death of you and your friends."

It was the last sentence that made Louie's blood turn cold. These were issues Louie knew he would have to deal with sooner rather than later and he was now more aware than ever.

The atmosphere had turned uneasy with Snow's last sentence. Louie knew it was down to him to try and be reassuring.

"Look I will be honest with everyone; I would be lying if I said I wasn't scared for all of us. I am. This is a very dangerous journey. We are up against extremely powerful magic from the underworld, but with that in mind, there is a slight chance we might just succeed in trying to save our worlds from the evil. It has to be better than sitting back and doing nothing.

"If we fail I would rather know in my heart that we tried our hardest to stop evil from taking over all that is good. We must all keep the thought of hope and fate in our minds and let this guide the decisions we find hard to make." Louie couldn't help but let out a sigh. "If we are going to be entering caves then we have to be as one with our senses. If any of us were to be taken by evil into the underworld, through a portal, our mission would be over. I would not be able to continue until we were all together again."

"You cannot have the entire journey rest on your shoulders," Summer began, "we all agreed to join you, Louie. No one sitting here was forced to come along. This is as much our burden as it is yours and I can only speak for myself but if I am captured by any evil creature I do not want you to stop this mission. You are to carry on. Don't underestimate our individual powers of survival, Louie. There wouldn't be much point in coming for me if all the worlds ended up being taken over by evil and there is more of a chance of that happening if you abandon the task set out."

The other friends all nodded in agreement.

"Louie. You have to stop trying to foresee what is ahead of us. This journey will unfold as it's meant to. It has all been written in the stars long before we existed and nothing we do will change what is meant to be." Louie looked at Petra as she spoke her wise words. She always managed to put Louie at ease when she spoke like this. "Now," she continued, "we need to get back on track to the cave of Saphical. Night is still upon us and if we can get there before daylight it might save us from other visitors. Julique will still think his sluth friend is tracking us. The map has shown a more direct route with the help of the tunnels within these iced walls."

After a while of studying the map Snow pointed the visitors in the direction of the exit and parted by simply saying two words, "Trust yourselves."

# Cave of Saphical

Settling into their journey, the group quickened the pace. In knowing that Julique could now be onto them made the snow easier somehow. Each stayed silent during the first mountain track they conquered. It was as if they were each thinking of the 'what ifs' regarding be captured or having to continue knowing that someone else was. This hit deep with Louie especially, but, if he was going to give this mission his all, he had to listen to Snow's warning and believe in himself to keep the friends he was growing to love, safe in his company.

Juggle was the first to break the silence. Being the leader on this trail, he was the first to see the crystal cave as he turned the final bend of the mountain path.

"Wow," he gasped.

The beauty of the cave was striking. The sun was starting to wake on the horizon. Its bright rays of first light bounced off the entrance to the cave catching the tips of crystal stones peeking from the mouth.

"It's beautiful," followed Tia.

They all stood and stared upon the cave, soaking in the morning sun.

Louie couldn't help but feel this day was lighter than the last, but he wondered, was this one of the cave's tricks to entice beings in? He then began to question his thoughts. Was he being negative with this thought or was he thinking ahead and being cleverer than the evil magic within? Louie shook his head to dismiss any thought at all. He was becoming confused and it wasn't helping.

"We're nearly there," Juggle continued, pointing to a snow-covered forest that lay below them. "Once we get past the valley down there it will take no time at all to climb up to the cave."

The forest had an eerie feel about it. Even though the sun was high the snow-covered trees leered over their path causing a colder atmosphere. There was no sound of creatures bustling around. In fact the forest was deathly silent until a loud roar was heard to echo from behind them. The friends quickened their pace until they felt they were far enough away from possibly meeting the creature that let out the roar. Juggle was the first to speed up his pace. He imagined a snow lion jumping out from the trees and this scared him half to death.

Eventually they stopped for a mid-morning snack at the base of the mountain that housed their intended destination.

The pit stop seemed quieter than the previous ones and it was obvious to them all the anticipation of what lay ahead was frightening to say the least.

Summer stood up. "We are nearly there and I think we should all remember what we are here to do. We have been set the task of finding Onyx's secrets about evil magic from her studies of Es'trixia, but we must also be aware that we may find ourselves directly on the path to the scroll of light and dark. If Julique and Es'trixia know we are here they will be trying to stop us no matter what. We are their only threat at the moment and we're walking into areas they know far better than we do."

Summer took a long sip of her luke-warm milk honey, then continued. "Onyx may not have even found the secret to the evil magic of Es'trixia so be aware that the paths she has put us on will lead to whatever it is she wanted us to see. No one is to break away from the group. We can't imagine what tricks have been set in the caves by either the elders or Julique so we are to stay together. Tia, do you still have that long piece of rope in your bag we used at Lake Owling?"

Tia reached into her bag and pulled out the piece of thin silkworm rope.

Summer took the rope and starting with Juggle she handed him one end. "Tie this round your waist, Juggle. Once we get to the mouth of the cave there may not be much time before we are seen, so we must be quick to fasten this piece of this rope to our bodies. If Juggle is at the rear of the group Louie should be at the front. Us girls should evenly distribute ourselves in between. Petra you should be next in line to Louie so you can guide him whilst holding the map. This will prevent us from being led astray. We need to be quiet from now on, in the hope we can enter undetected. It's important we remember we have nothing to lose and everything to gain if we manage to find what we are looking for."

Louie felt proud to be with Summer on this journey. She had managed to somehow calm them all with her wise but honest words.

It was a quick trek up to the mouth of the cave. Once outside they hid behind a boulder whilst they did as Summer had suggested and tied the rope so they were all connected.

The mouth of the cave was large, considerably larger than it looked from the valley. The crystals, though also large, didn't sparkle as much up close; in fact they looked more like jagged blue rocks bursting out in all directions.

Before moving into the cave Petra took the map out of her pocket and placed it on the floor in front of where they were all crouched. The map now showed the inside of the cave.

"Once we are in we need to stay to the left side," she whispered, "which takes us to some steps."

"We have just climbed this mountain and now you're telling me we have to go back down?" Juggle slumped in his crouched position, unhappy with what the map was showing. His wings were really cramped and his body felt tired.

"Juggle," Petra started, "we have come this far and only now you start complaining!"

Louie chipped in, "It's just a few more steps, Jugg."

Louie being at the front now checked his rope tie. "Is everyone ready? On three we are all to get onto our feet and follow me into the cave. Once we are in we will stay to the left and then Petra will tell me if and when I need to change direction. Are we all clear? Any questions?" No one spoke. "OK. One, two, three."

As quick as they could, each one followed instructions. Louie led everyone into the cave keeping as tight to the outer wall as he could to keep camouflaged.

They now stood inside the much awaited cave of Saphical.

# Fallen angel

"Have we any news from the sluth yet?" Es'trixia belted out from across the room to Julique as she strolled casually in through the usual arch. "Surely not more minions have failed you? Do they not have any respect for who you are?"

Knowing she was probably treading on thin ice with the mood Julique was in, Es'trixia couldn't help herself. This had gone far enough in her mind and they didn't have time to mess around with amateurs any longer.

"If you can't be trusted to pick the correct creatures for this job you should allow me to take over."

"Absolutely not!" screamed Julique, at the top of his voice. He turned around from a balcony he was standing on that looked out over a black sea of flames and molten lava.

Es'trixia was taken by surprise when Julique turned to face her. His eyes were blacker than earlier and face thinner. Was this through the stress he was under to get his hands on the scroll or was it a further transformation towards the darker side of evil? She was unsure and hoped it wasn't the latter of the two.

If he was turning darker it meant he was a match for her powers, if he knew how to use them. Realising quickly she would have to play this his way, she nodded as she stood now in front of him and decided on a calmer voice.

"I trust your judgment, Julique, but we have very little time now and my sources have no more information about the young group. They seemed to have disappeared. Maybe we need to rethink our game." Es'trixia took Julique's hand and led him to his throne where she sat him down. Es'trixia continued, "The awguls were sent to hunt the scroll out from where we thought it was last buried by the sisters, between Verlum and Tarania. They had no luck and it would seem that it is no longer where we thought.

"The next step was to find a clue to its whereabouts so we sent more awguls to Onyx's cottage where we discovered, through my sources, that a group of youngsters were also at the cottage looking for something of Onyx's, but we are not sure what exactly. So at the moment, the only thing we have gained is information that suggests the gods and angels are up to something."

Es'trixia swayed on the spot as she spoke. "From there we decided to find this group of youngsters and kill them, which would have made our lives a bit easier knowing there was no one else on the same track as us. Once again we are still in no better position to proceed as the awguls from Onyx's cottage didn't return and so far the sluth has not reported back with any news of the youngsters' deaths. Ummmm, the end result at the moment being we are no closer to finding out the resting place of the scroll and the eclipse will soon be here. We had better start thinking of the next step, Julique."

Julique's face started to relax as he calmed down from his outburst. "If they have disappeared I am guessing that they are no longer in Verlum or Tarania. What contacts do you have in Herbeya?"

"I like your thinking, but I have none. It was the only land that seemed full of anti-evil magic. But I know that there are ways in through the caves. I have never had the need to use them so can't help you there."

"Yes there are a few entrances. I used to use one of them. That was a very long time ago it would be impossible to enter through the portal without alarming the elders."

Julique sat up in the throne remembering the elders had made it easy for themselves to enter the underworld undetected through the caves. "I will find out where the others are and then I think the only way to continue is to carry out these tasks ourselves."

He looked at Estrixa who was just about to scoff at the idea of herself doing any dirty work, but she withheld her reaction with calmness and nodded in agreement.

"I will return to you when you have the details of our excursion out of this hell hole. Meanwhile I will look to find a way of cloaking us so we can enter undetected, though it may not be long lasting."

Es'trixia walked away quickly, hoping she had done enough to convince Julique she was there to help him.

# The Doorway

The cave was dark and colder than the outside air. The dark blue crystal walls were uneven and sharp; on the tips of the jagged spikes that poked out in all directions hung frozen droplets. Being cautious where he stepped Louie listened to every command Petra made. He led the line along the same wall for miles, through tight holes and over uneven ground. Louie, being the first in line, was also the first to find the spear-like crystals that stuck out from the wall catching his back and arms, slicing through his feathered coat. Every now and then he felt his warm blood trickle on his body from the cuts he was collecting.

Puddles of once-melted ice reflected the deep blue colour of the walls and ceiling, keeping them from having to find another source of light. It didn't take long for their eyes to adjust to their surroundings. The sounds within the cave echoed, magnifying the dripping of melting snow coupled with the rumbling of the rocks.

"Stop here," Petra whispered. "The map is showing the steps are only a few strides away. Once we reach them we have to be extra careful not to pull

197

each other over when descending. The map isn't showing me how many steps there are or even how far down we'll be going. You will have to use your instinct, Louie, until the map changes. Extra care though," Petra warned. "It seems the walls around us are getting shorter and the ceiling is getting lower."

"OK. I'm going to go slow until I reach them. Is everyone still in line behind me?"

Petra turned around and checked the queue behind her then answered for all of them. "Yes, we're all ready. Good luck."

Louie took three careful steps. On his fourth he felt the ground slant away from his foot. He stopped and pushed his foot forward until it dropped off the ledge.

The direction they'd taken had led them all into a tight tunnel. Louie felt himself hunched over more so than before.

His foot lowered onto the first step. He bent down and used his hand to judge how deep the steps were before he moved his other foot.

"Petra, tell the others that the steps are quite deep and they may need to put both feet onto one step before going onto the next to help with balance. It seems to be a tight spiral of steps."

Petra passed the message on and waited for Louie to move onto the second step before she stepped onto the first.

It took no time at all before the six friends were in a rhythm of walking down the steps. Being the last in line, Juggle counted seventy-two steps before he heard Petra whisper that Louie had reached a flat area. It was a minute or two before he had the final step in sight and without any warning the moment his foot left the final step, the ground opened up and swallowed the spiral stairs. Juggle hurled himself towards his friends to avoid being sucked into the hole and landed hard on the ground wincing at the pain that shot through his body.

A cloud of dust from the crumbling rock filled the air before it was also sucked in and the hole closed.

The group stood coughing and spluttering trying to inhale clean air into their lungs and catching their breath at the same time.

Louie was the first to recover.

He was now standing in a crescent-shaped cave with three crooked doorways that appeared to be engraved into the rocky wall. Each door had a different coloured crystal outlining. The first was orange like amber, the middle one was emerald and the last was rose quartz pink.

"What does the map show now, P?" Louie asked, slightly confused.

"It just shows these three doors."

All six gathered around the map and watched the word 'INSTINCT' flash up and fade away.

"Instinct?" Tia questioned. "Well that doesn't help very much, does it?"

"No, but," Summer replied, "I think it is asking us to make the choice."

"Louie," Petra began, "my instinct is telling me that you are the one who needs to make this choice."

"Me?" he replied stepping back slightly from the circle they had made. "I can't make this decision on my own. We're all here together." Louie shook his head as he spoke. "If I make the wrong choice I could put us all in danger."

"That's the point, Louie. Remember what Snow said to us before we left him? Trust!"

"Why don't you get your staff out, Louie," Squidge suggested. "It may help you to decide."

Louie looked at all his companions and waited a moment before reaching into his satchel.

Holding the staff in his hand he stared at it for a while wondering how to work it. He stepped towards the three doors holding the staff out in front and waited for something to happen, feeling a fool as he did so.

"See. Nothing is happening."

"Give it a chance," replied Petra, "maybe you have to focus on what you want it to do."

Louie repositioned his feet, hoping that might help and lifted the staff into the air. He closed his eyes and tried to focus on the doors in front of him.

Unbeknown to Louie the staff started to glow yellow. The five bystanders watched in amazement.

"It's working, Louie," whispered Summer. "Whatever you're doing is working."

Louie began to feel a warm sensation rush through his body as his mind became more focused. 'Which door should I choose?' he murmured in his mind. Louie jumped when he heard a reply.

"Three," the voice said.

Opening his eyes in disbelief he turned back to his audience.

"Did you hear that?"

"Hear what, Louie?" Juggle replied.

"The voice that answered my question!"

"There has been no voice."

Louie felt slightly spooked. "I asked the question 'What door should I choose?' and a voice replied as loud as I am speaking now, 'Three'!"

"Only you heard the voice, Louie," Tia stated.

"Well if that's what you heard then that is the door we will be taking. We trust you, Louie," Petra said walking over to him. "Lead the way and we will follow."

Placing her hands on his shoulders she turned him to face the door and nudged him in its direction.

Louie stood in front of the rose quartz door and put his hand on the round handle. His stomach turned with nerves as he twisted it and pushed the door open.

There was a suction of cold air, taking his breath away then the door continued to open on its own.

Nothing but darkness.

"Shall we go through?" Louie questioned.

"Yes," Petra replied, "we have made our choice."

Louie took the first step into the darkness, quickly followed by the others. The first thing that hit them all was the strong smell of burning. Huddled together they moved forward into the unknown. The darkness started to lift the further forward they moved. A striking purple haze grew in the distance and waved from one side of the cave to the other. Although an unusual sight, the group edged their way towards it. Somehow the sight didn't feel threatening. More to the point they had nowhere else to go.

A faint sound of humming could be heard the closer the haze moved until it stopped.

"What is it?" Petra whispered in Louie's ear.

"I have no idea." Taking another step forward Louie felt himself being pulled towards the soft humming. His body became relaxed and he could hear nothing else but the humming. Standing still Louie's feet felt like lead. He couldn't move but at the same time didn't want to go any further. His mind became blank and the more he tried to speak the less he could move his lips.

"Louie? Louie can you hear me?" Petra now felt concerned, yet couldn't get an answer.

Petra noticed a glazed look in his eyes and, waving her hand in front of his face, got no response. She started shaking his shoulders, still nothing.

"There is something wrong with Louie; he seems to be in some sort of trance."

Getting no response from anyone else Petra turned to repeat what she had said when she saw that the rest of the group were in the same state.

"What is going on?" she questioned. "Summer? Tia? Snap out of it. This can't be happening!"

Petra turned to the haze and saw a transformation happening in the centre of it. An erratic energy shot out bolts of purple lightning in their direction followed by a pulsating cloud of purple stones every few moments. Petra now felt in danger, the bolts of lightning seemed to be extending, becoming closer.

Louie, Tia, Squidge, Juggle and Summer started to walk forward towards the haze. The humming sound was now louder, sounding very similar to a lullaby, sung by a soft voice. The sound was spooky.

Petra tugged at the rope, that attached them all, in an attempt to get them away from the haze but she wasn't strong enough. There seemed to be a magnetic pull towards the energy cloud. The lightning show was now intense and the humming deafening. She couldn't think properly with all the noise. It didn't help that the cave echoed the sound. Petra had to focus but it was impossible. The others were practically stepping into it now, pulling her in with them.

"Louie's staff." Petra leaned forward and grabbed the staff hanging out of his bag. It burnt her hand as she touched it but she ignored the pain. She put it in Louie's hand and held it out in front of him. Instantly the staff glowed white and a beam of light projected onto the haze and seemed to burn into it. The lightning was now struggling to protrude from the centre. The haze began to spin frantically causing a rush of air to circulate in the room, then with a gasping sound the air sucked itself into a small purple ball before dulling.

The cave was silent. Petra started to see her friends shake out of the trance and return to normal. She let out a sigh of relief and heard something fall onto the ground. With the little light she had she looked down and lying there on the floor was a purple stone.

"An amethyst?" she said to herself as she got up off the floor. Now ignoring her friends as they started to question what had happened, Petra reached down and picked the amethyst stone up. It felt warm.

"What just happened?" Summer asked before anyone else had a chance.

"The haze," Petra answered still studying what she had found, "it put you all into some sort of trance. You were all about to step into it and were taking me with you."

"What are you holding, P?" asked Squidge.

"When the haze disappeared this was left in its place."

"Wow, it looks like an amethyst. They are very powerful in Verlum. We use them to reflect any evil."

Petra then began to remember what she had read about this type of stone. "I remember reading about these. We don't have them in Tarania. Something to do with the power of the gods repelling such a force."

"Yes that would be correct," Squidge confirmed, "the amethyst is a stone of the angels. It signifies peace and calm but also has a reverse effect on the gods because they are mainly the bearers of strength and courage. It has been said that when the gods were in the vicinity of these stones, they would become almost too strong and less forgiving, causing most of them to ignore the thought of calmness. When the lands were joined the gods at that time ordered for the stones to be taken from their land and put in Verlum where the angels would use them in the way they should be used. The balance of the worlds had changed and the gods knew that they were unbalanced because the angels had been separated from them.

Tarania would have been a very angry place if the stones had of been left without the goodness of the angels' auras to keep the calmness and peace within them."

"Your staff, Louie, saved us all, you know. Even though I must say I didn't appreciate the burn it gave me when I touched it."

Petra began to feel the burn in her hand and it stung.

Tia saw the burn and got her pot of ointment out and rubbed it on Petra's injury. "Thank you, P, for saving us."

"OK. So we now have a purple stone. What are we supposed to do with it?"

Juggle held it in his hand feeling the weight and holding it up to the little light they could see with.

Squidge continued, "I'm guessing we take it with us. If we've been lucky enough to find one in Herbeya it may be something we need to help work out the secret of Es'trixia. But I am only guessing. It is strange that we have managed to escape the haze and gain a crystal."

"What's the map saying, P?" asked Louie.

Peering down at the map Petra could just about make out the dark lines the map was making in the poor light. "It seems we can only carry straight on ahead; it's showing nothing more than a straight path."

The six friends checked they were still tied to each other, then carried along the same path for a long while. The cave didn't change in appearance and it was hard to judge just how far they'd been walking, though they all knew they were being led deeper into the core of the cave.

Louie wondered why they had only been met by one force of magic so far. They had spent nearly a whole day trudging through the cave and so far the magic, whether good or evil, had been limited. Not that he was complaining, it was just a concern that didn't seem to sit right in his mind.

# The Opening

Es'trixia put a few bottles of potion in her cloak and had one last glance in the book she kept on a stand in the corner of her room. She really needed to stay in Julique's good books just until she had him out of the underworld and the whereabouts of the scroll in her midst. Es'trixia hated being nice to anyone, but most of all an angel, no matter if he was darker than the rest. But, she had something he didn't and Julique was never going to know what it was. Actually she thought to herself no one knew what her greatest weapon was and, by the time they would realise, she would be ruling all of the worlds and it would be too late for any of them to do anything about it. She smiled to herself and closed the door to her room locking it with a magic spell as always.

Julique, trustingly, drank the potion Es'trixia handed to him. "This will get us through the elders' door undetected. It will start to wear off after a while but we should have enough potions to last us until we have found what we need."

Julique winced at the taste of the revolting brew she had concocted.

They held hands and vanished from Julique's lair.

Es'trixia and Julique reappeared moments later, stood in another cave that felt a lot cooler than they were used to. Julique let go of Es'trixia's hand as soon as he could. They were at a dead end. Julique stepped ahead of Estrixa and opened his thinly feathered wings to full span.

His wings, although dark, now had a silver outline around them. He closed his eyes and stood silently still. Nothing happened until his wings closed and took a step back. On the wall in front of them the rocks shifted. A black granite doorway appeared.

Julique put his hand on the door and took a deep breath, readily awaiting the push he had avoided for what felt an eternity. He would soon be under the radar of the elders if this potion failed to work.

This could be the end for him.

# Dark Meets Light

The friends kept their spirits up by talking quietly to one another along the jiggery, winding path. The cave was now misty on the ground making it harder for Louie to find his footing.

They discussed family, friends and school, exchanging stories of their teachers and classmates.

Petra, although joining in the conversations, kept checking the map eagerly awaiting another sign to the next part of the journey.

Soon the friends became quiet again. The atmosphere changed all of a sudden. The air felt thick with darkness, almost clammy on their skins making their breathing hard work.

Though the feathered coats were still keeping them from feeling the cold, they were also becoming heavy as the clamminess set in. The humidity weighed the feathers down. Juggle stopped to unbutton his coat.

Upon stopping, it gave them all a chance to catch their breath. It was then that Louie realised that the staff popping out of his satchel had been neglected for that entire part of their journey. He took it out of his bag and held it once again, still weary of its power.

Touching it he again felt a surge of warmth rush through his veins. Something instantly felt wrong.

"We need to be careful," he said calmly, "something feels wrong." His stomach fluttered now with nerves. The feeling was becoming stronger as he continued, "I don't know what the staff it trying to tell me but it is giving me a warning that danger is close."

With those words Petra looked down at the map and saw they were now in front of another doorway. By the time she looked up to see if the map was correct, the wall they had failed to see ahead started to transform into a black granite door.

"There's another door," Petra pointed ahead, but held back. She too had a bad feeling come over her.

"Stay back," Louie whispered loudly, holding his arm out to stop them moving forward any further.

With those words the door flew open and stood in the doorway was a female and an angel.

# No Going Back

Their eyes met and for a split moment everyone froze. Thinking quickly Louie pointed his staff at the angel, who he guessed was Julique.

A bubble instantly cocooned the group of friends. Es'trixia pushed Julique out of her way at the same time and forced an energy ball in Louie's direction. She was too late: the bubble was up and around them.

Everything was moving at such a quick pace. The energy balls and fire bounced off the bubble and backfired into the wall close to Julique causing part of the wall to crumble. Julique then tried with a shot of fire from his hands, having the same effect.

The group of friends stood close together ducking the shots and at the same time using their individual skills of combat by firing back with their own energy missiles.

Julique and Es'trixia flew out of the doorway quicker than light. Both took a different area of the bubble to attack and were attacking to kill.

Es'trixia was enjoying the challenge and knew she would only have to strike the same point of the bubble shield a few times before she would eventually have her first victim dead.

The area they all stood in was frantic. Louie didn't know what way to turn. They were trapped.

At that moment of panic Louie realised what he was seeing: the doorway it was free. Nothing was standing in the way. Louie managed to grab Summer's wrist to let her know his plan. She looked in the direction, quickly glancing without anyone noticing between fireballs and ice bolts being thrown. Petra heard Louie's thoughts and had already prepared Juggle and Tia. Squidge would be carried.

Summer was quick to grab a smoke ball from her bag and threw it at Julique's feet. The air instantly turned into a thick grey cloud. The friends couldn't see one another any more.

Upon creating the smokescreen Summer grabbed Louie's arm and dragged him and her five friends past the evil two and in through the door. Before they knew it they had become separated from the rope and were running for their lives into a dark tunnel. The grey cloud started to evaporate away from them un-clinging its thickness from their clothes.

"It's Julique," Summer shouted as she ran, "we must keep the bubble around us for as long as we can. He will kill us."

"Es'trixia has weakened the bubble," Louie replied.

Juggle stayed at the back and kept checking behind him. "How long will the smokescreen last?"

"Not long enough," Summer replied.

"We have to find somewhere to hide," Tia added, barely being able to breathe.

"We're in their world now." Managing to glance at the map once again Petra saw the words UNDERWORLD flashing rapidly in front of her eyes. "We are in trouble, guys, we've entered the underworld."

"What?" Juggle questioned, screeching at the top of his voice in disbelief. "Is that map trying to get us killed?"

"We need a plan. I have no idea what we should do." Louie needed to stop and think but there was no time.

"Just keep the bubble up, Louie. It's the only plan we have." Squidge was being carried by Louie who had scooped her up midway.

They were no longer in a tunnel. They seemed to have entered a completely different world.

The tunnel led them to an opening that widened enormously into a land housing petrified trees and boulders of burning rock coupled with molten liquid being spat out from sporadic holes in the ground. In the distance dark shadows of mountains added to the heaviness of the land. Ghostly figures, of different beings, frantically flew high above the group, some swooping down trying to attack their bubble of protection. The dark sky flashed red and to their left a sea of angry black waves rolled thick like treacle.

The ground they were running on was ash-coloured and slippery in places.

There was nothing close by that would allow them to seek refuge which meant they would be out in the open for some time hoping their protection would last until they struck lucky. The ghosts were not helping and the bubble flickered weaker every time they were hit.

An emerald whirlwind hit the ground ahead and darted towards them fast.

No matter which direction they turned there was no way of avoiding the inevitable. They really were doomed this time with no way out at all.

The whirlwind picked up speed and span into a tornado.

Instinctively they turned to run but it was too late for anything, the six friends were sucked up by the tornado along with whatever else was on the ground with them. Tossed and turned, they were thrashed against one another at speed.

Louie's bubble had well and truly evaporated and there was no chance of him conjuring another one whilst being spun around in mid-air and thrown from one side of the tornado to the other. He looked up to the top and saw an eye. It was the same eye he had rebelled at Lake Owling but this time the eye was the winner.

"You cannot win against my powers, you silly little creatures. Look at you now. You literally walked into my hands." A female's voice laughed uncontrollably. "Will I kill you now or later? I just can't decide." Es'trixia's cackle continued. The eye disappeared.

The tornado took all six youngsters higher into the sky and over the black sea of death that housed the dead souls of evil. Giant serpents could be seen slithering in and out of the waves. Juggle, upon seeing this, was sick with fright expecting to be dropped into the sea any moment. But that wasn't her plan. Es'trixia tightened her grip on the tornado making it spin faster until finally it stopped abruptly at the balcony of Julique's cave. The friends struggled with force but couldn't move; they were now suspended in the air. Then, without warning only four were spat out individually, keeping Louie and Squidge captive.

Summer, Tia, Juggle and Petra hit the razor-sharp serrated wall of Julique's lair, hard.

Immediately they were imprisoned into one of the corners and, to stop them escaping, a curtain of hot molten liquid cascaded from the ceiling to the floor like a waterfall.

The impact of hitting the wall caused some agonising injuries. Summer had been stabbed with a sharp spear of ice, and the tip had stuck in her right thigh. They huddled together and didn't move. Summer managed to rip the spear from her leg before anyone else noticed, though her silver-coloured blood poured out fast.

Louie and Squidge were now upside down in the air, still controlled by Es'trixia; she made sure they knew their place. She bashed their bodies against the cave walls like they were rotten carcasses. Es'trixia was now in sight and walking behind her new guests escorting them to a separate room.

"You just don't know how lucky I feel right now," she said practically dancing with joy, "a scruffin and a god, it must be my lucky day."

Once inside the room she stood and thought about where to put them. Almost agreeing with her own thoughts, she nodded and opened another door that looked like a wardrobe.

With one flick of her hand Louie and Squidge were flung into mid-air and chucked through the wardrobe doors. The doors slammed shut and Es'trixia left the room.

# Strange Findings

"Squidge, are you OK? Speak to me, Squidge."

"I'm in one piece I think, but I'm bruised."

"I think my leg is broken," Louie groaned. "I don't think I can move any more."

"Just stay still while I try and get some light in here." Squidge lifted herself gently up off the floor and walked cautiously around the room feeling the walls, until her paws touched what felt like a shutter. Bingo, there behind the shutter was a tiny window secured with molten-hot bars keeping anything from breaking in or escaping, but it was enough. Opening the shutter slowly the room gulped a glow of orange light.

Squidge turned and looked around. Louie's leg was very swollen but Squidge didn't think it was broken. Louie, though in pain, had other more pressing things to focus his mind on and tried his hardest to push the feeling out of his mind.

Squidge stood back up after her examination of Louie's leg and slowly searched the room with her eyes. It was then that she noticed something across the other side of the room: a girl with long black hair slumped in a rocking chair with her hands and feet tied. There was no movement at all.

"Oh my... Louie... Look... another prisoner."

Louie looked over his shoulder and instantly forgot the pain in his leg. Slightly hesitant, he too picked himself off the floor and slowly hobbled over to the chair. On reaching the chair his foot kicked a large clear rock. Louie looked down and saw that there was, in fact, a number of these rocks surrounding the chair. Carefully he leaned in towards the girl and placed his hand on her shoulder. He gave her a nudge.

Nothing. Not a single flinch of movement.

Louie not entirely sure if his nudge was sufficient nudged the girl harder. Still nothing.

"Squidge... I think she is dead."

"Oh no, that's awful." Squidge joined Louie in peering at the girl. Fumbling around in her tummy bag she pulled out a sliver of mirror and held it under the girl's nose. The mirror misted up. "She's not dead," Squidge said with relief.

"What's wrong with her then? Surely she isn't asleep." Louie gave yet another nudge but this time it turned into more of a shake.

"Maybe she's under a spell."

"Squidge what are these rocks placed around her?"

Squidge looked down. "They look like opal rocks." She scratched her furry head as she looked back up at the girl and again down onto the ground. "I know all there is to know about rocks, gems and crystals but I have never seen such large opal rocks before and I couldn't imagine why they would be around this girl. Opals are known as the gem of the gods and are thought to bring bad luck to those not worthy of it. You see, they can soak up knowledge from anything. Usually they are stored and later drained when the knowledge is needed."

Squidge moved one of the rocks to one side.

There was movement from the girl's left hand.

"Look, Squidge, did you see that? She moved her hand when you moved the rock."

Squidge moved another rock and the girl moved her left leg.

"I think the rocks are keeping the girl captive, Squidge. Quick, move all of them away from her."

Squidge and Louie swept the opals away, scattering them across the floor. The girl was now waking slowly.

She started by lifting her head. Louie and Squidge edged back to give her some room as she opened her eyes.

Louie got his dagger from his bag and cut the ties from around her wrists and ankles.

The girl was older than Louie and very beautiful. She raised her hand to her head and rubbed it. Looking up she stared at the boy and the scruffin standing before her. The girl smiled.

# Awakening

There was no introduction. The girl seemed to be alert almost straight away.

"Thank you. If you're here with me it means you have obviously met Es'trixia. She will be back soon to check on you. We have to be quick with a plan." The girl loosened the ties from her wrists and ankles as she spoke.

"Who are you and why were you asleep in here?" Louie helped the girl stand up from the chair assisting her in gaining the strength in her legs again. "How long have you been here?"

"I am Onyx."

"Oh my," Squidge gasped, taking a wobbly step back with shock.

"I have been captured in this room by Es'trixia for over a hundred years. I was close to getting the answer to dark magic when I fell into a trap she'd set. Since then she has held me prisoner and used my knowledge of magic to fuel her own power. dark magic needs good magic for it to work, Es'trixia has used me to become very powerful, managing to gain all the knowledge I had on magic but, so far, failed to gain the knowledge of the scroll.

"This was her only wish when she captured me and thought that the resting place of the scroll would eventually transfer into the opals you moved once the other information had been transferred. Little did she know that I had locked the scroll's whereabouts away in the back of my mind with the help of the elders during my meditation messages. I just hope that the last pieces of knowledge have not yet transferred."

Onyx stretched her arms above her head then behind her back before continuing to explain more in a rushed voice.

"If you are here it means you followed my clues and the eclipse is upon us. We must get to the resting place of the scroll immediately and take it to your father, Louie. It will be safe with him and the leader of the angels. But, first we need to stop Es'trixia. I am no match for her powers now so it will take all our efforts to slow her down. I have a good idea of how we do this.

Onyx quickly explained her plan, and then returned to her chair. Squidge closed the shutter and joined Louie on the ground. The three waited for Es'trixia's return.

It wasn't long before Es'trixia stepped in through the wardrobe doors. She was instantly struck by a spell chanted by Onyx. Louie hit her with his staff sending her to the floor. He continued using his staff holding it to her head.

Es'trixia became limp and began shaking uncontrollably. The staff glowed green until a light shot out from the top hitting Es'trixia in the forehead. Lying lifeless on the floor a green energy covered her body like a coffin.

Squidge, Louie and Onyx ran out of the wardrobe and into her room. Onyx couldn't resist grabbing Es'trixia's spell book as she ran past and, in doing so, said a spell that shrank it to pocket size.

The next hurdle was Julique. Onyx wasn't worried about him and his powers. After what he did to her father she would gladly put him in limbo for the rest of eternity and take great pleasure in doing so.

They ran into Julique's lair through the arch usually used by Es'trixia.

Taken by surprise Julique jumped from his throne and shot a spray of ice and fire towards Louie. Louie tumbled to the ground.

"Don't stop!" he shouted to Squidge who was running back to help him.

Squidge ignored Louie and helped drag him up off the floor as much as she could. Louie struggled to stand but managed to find his footing. At the same time he pointed his staff at Julique who was now taking great pleasure in aiming at Onyx.

Julique had realised who she was immediately. He smiled as he shot a second round at Onyx, he missed. Onyx chanted a few words. His throne lifted up and flew straight into his back, knocking him to the floor.

At the same time Squidge left Louie and ran over to the waterfall of molten lava that was being guarded by a small troll like creature. Squidge ran at the troll with all her force pushing the troll under the molten liquid. The molten lava engulfed the troll stopping the flow. The troll let out a deathly scream before vanishing into a pool of molten sludge.

Summer, Juggle, Tia and Petra ran out from their cell. Immediately all six friends and Onyx were fighting Julique and his minions. The battle of fire, ice and magic was intense. Onyx shouted at Louie to get his friends in a group. They huddled together in a corner fighting off anything that came towards them.

Onyx gave Julique one last blast of magic sending him into the air. As Julique descended back down towards the ground one of his wings caught on a jagged piece of ice protruding from the wall. Julique screamed in agony, arching his back with the pain and hung unable to move.

Onyx ran to the group of youngsters and on joining hands disappeared from the lair.

'Nooooooo…!' Julique shouted in anger.

# The Resting Place

The landing was kinder than the previous. The field looked familiar. Louie stood in a field full of luminous flowers. The moon was high feeding the field with light.

Each friend looked injured in some way. They took off their feathered coats to cool down, after all they were back in a warmer place.

"Where are we?" Louie asked.

"We're back in Verlum. Look." Tia pointed to the edge of the forest to their right. "The unicorns, they are still cloaked."

The three unicorns Tia had cloaked were grazing in the same place they had left them days before.

Onyx brushed herself down and reached into her cloak pocket. "Es'trixia's book of magic," she whispered to herself, "finally."

"Who are you?" asked Juggle.

"I'm Onyx."

Summer, Petra and Tia gasped when they heard her name.

"I can't thank you enough for trusting my map and for saving my life. We have to move though, Es'trixia will eventually gain consciousness and

Julique, I imagine, is already planning his next move."

"Surely we are safe in Verlum? They can't enter," Summer asked.

"They can enter. Es'trixia has my knowledge of cloaking spells and has already sourced ingredients for them. Once they realise where we are, we will all be in danger. My magic is no match for hers at the moment. The eclipse is later today and the sun is due to rise soon."

"What do we have to do?" Summer continued.

"We have to get the scroll and place it on safe ground."

"But I thought it was hidden from evil."

"It was until Es'trixia started looking into all of my thoughts. Though she has never seen the final resting place, she has seen my sisters and I within the vicinity. It won't take much for her to piece the places together and find the scroll. Louie, I will share a unicorn with you, everyone else follow."

The unicorns flew high above the clouds. Louie had forgotten just how magical it felt to be on one. Onyx took control guiding the unicorn through canyons and over rivers. She was quick to change direction every few miles as if shaking off anyone following.

The sun had started to rise on the horizon; it was a beautiful sight to see after the ordeal Louie and his friends had been through. Louie felt as though he had not seen the daylight for an eternity and basked in the new light that was hitting his face. Louie wanted to asked Onyx so much, but felt this was not the time or the place. He knew now this journey was the most important of all and probably the most dangerous.

Onyx began to prepare the unicorn for landing. The descent was quick and very skilled. The unicorn seemed to know exactly what was expected of him. The unicorns followed the leader and landed in a desert.

Summer was confused: she hadn't seen this part of Verlum before. In fact she didn't even know Verlum had a desert.

The land was hot with no breeze. The sun, though only just peeking over the horizon, was stifling. The heatwaves danced in the distance.

Onyx helped Louie down from their unicorn. "We must hurry. Louie, take the god's staff out of your satchel and keep it in your hands. You are the only one that can give us warning if evil is close."

Louie did as he was told without question.

"Squidge," Summer started, "did you know Verlum had desert land?"

"No."

"Tia, did you know about it?"

"Not at all. I can't believe we didn't know about this. We have studied all maps covering Verlum."

"You wouldn't have seen it on any map," Onyx interrupted, whilst pacing through the hot sand. "We asked that when the lands were joined and the border formed, all maps hid this area and you will soon see why."

The group followed every step Onyx took. They were all sweating intensely. The friends looked a sight for sore eyes. Not one of them walked comfortably. Each one had received an injury of some sort but knew they couldn't slow down.

Juggle was dripping with sweat. He was already down to just his T-shirt.

Onyx stopped and stood for a moment in silence with her eyes closed and arms out to her side. Louie and summer felt relief for a moment's rest. Squidge noticed blood running down Summer's leg and, when she acknowledged it, Summer tried to brush it off as just a scratch. Squidge ignored the game of bravery and quickly tied a tourniquet above the gash to slow the bleeding.

Meanwhile Juggle continued to strip down to just shorts; he couldn't bear the heat although he was so pleased they were out of the cold.

"How are your wings, Juggle?" asked Tia.

"Sore," he replied trying to stretch the first initial injury out. "How are you? I saw you get hit by an energy ball back in Julique's lair."

"Sore," she replied with a smile. The two of them laughed at their injuries.

Onyx dropped her arms and opened her eyes. In the distance a pyramid rose up from the sand. Onyx walked forward, followed by everyone else.

The pyramid, though tall, stayed discreet due to its sand-coloured exterior. The heat helped by blurring the vision with its wave of heat. A large section at the base of the pyramid slid open allowing Onyx and her followers to walk into a huge square area.

Blazing torches lined each wall and lit up one after the other until all were awake and burning. When the firelight had woken the room, a blue and orange mosaic path could be seen leading directly to the centre where there stood a podium with a glass case upon it.

"I will continue to the podium in the centre. You must all stay here because we set magic traps too dangerous for you all to avoid. I will collect the scroll from the glass cabinet, then we will immediately make our way to Tarania. Whatever happens stay off this path and stay silent," Onyx warned.

The friends watched in anticipation as Onyx stepped onto the path and slowly made her way towards the glass cabinet.

Louie couldn't help but think this was the longest path he had ever seen.

The steps she took were unusual, changing from lunges, over certain areas, to small short steps in others. There certainly didn't seem to be a rhythm to them.

Finally landing on the podium, Onyx placed her hands on the cabinet which, in turn, started to glow gold.

Louie, so engrossed, had completely forgotten to keep an eye on his staff. With that thought he peered down at his hands and his blood turned cold.

"Evil!" he shouted.

Onyx stopped immediately and turned to look at Louie. It was too late: she couldn't stop the scroll from being uncovered from the glass casing, It was out in the open now.

She quickly grabbed the tubular case and turned to leave the podium but, there in front of her, hovering above the path, was Es'trixia. She glanced at the others who were now pinned against the pyramid wall by their throats.

"Thank you, Onyx," Es'trixia began, "you have done everything I hoped you would do, although I didn't expect such a fight I must say." Es'trixia held something in her hand. It was Louie's staff. Onyx couldn't risk moving now Es'trixia had that.

"There is nowhere to go, is there? I win. I now have the scroll and will have you as my servant. The 'All-Powerful Es'trixia' is what you will call me when I have stood in front of the eclipse."

"You don't have the scroll yet, Es'trixia," Onyx replied with gritted teeth.

"Mmm true, hand it to me now."

"You will have to kill me first."

"And where is the fun in that?"

Julique watched Es'trixia hovering in front of the scroll. He knew he would have no chance of any power if she got hold of it first. Thinking quickly he formed a bridge of water between himself and Es'trixia. Before she realised what was happening Julique was at her side. Es'trixia had no use for him any more and on seeing him next to her she became enraged.

"I will take the scroll, Es'trixia, and will keep it safe until the eclipse," Julique said reaching out towards Onyx.

Es'trixia turned to face Julique which gave Onyx the only opportunity to get away.

Louie felt helpless. It was all his fault. Onyx asked him to carry out one task. He couldn't watch the outcome of this scene; Es'trixia would soon be holding the scroll which meant Louie had failed. He closed his eyes in shame until he was forced to open them again. Something tugged on his foot.

Peering down Louie saw Tyke, the scruffin, standing below him.

"Shhhhh," Tyke hushed. He slowly pulled something out of his tummy bag. It was another staff.

He reached up as far as he could, to Louie, and put the staff in his hand. Tyke then disappeared.

Louie's body surged with power. Placing the staff on the electric rope, gripping his neck, he broke it and fell to the floor. He continued along the line until all his friends were free.

Julique and Es'trixia were oblivious to what was happening, due to their petty arguing.

Louie stood with his friends behind him. He pointed the staff in Es'trixa's direction and for the first time asked the staff to hit her with its power. The staff did just that. Catching Es'trixia off guard she was thrown across the large open area hitting the floor face first.

Onyx took this opportunity to escape and sprinted back over the path she had so cautiously stepped on moments earlier. The path crumbled under her feet as she ran. Jumping onto solid ground she continued to run out the pyramid towards the unicorns.

Julique, also caught off guard, instinctively lifted off the ground to take flight, but was swiftly reminded that his wings were injured when he hit the sand with a thud.

The six friends followed Onyx as quickly as they could. Es'trixia was up again and screaming with rage. Louie turned to see if she was behind them. 'Not yet,' he thought.

When they reached the unicorns the sky was starting to turn dark. The eclipse was beginning.

"Can we not just disappear from here?" Louie shouted to Onyx.

"No, we're too late. Magic weakens with an eclipse. We must hurry and get to the bridge that joins Tarania and Verlum."

Up in the air, they flew faster than before. Es'trixia was gaining on them fast. She had obviously regained her strength back after the fall.

The unicorns flapped their wings as fast as they could, but Louie felt this was still not fast enough. He turned back around in the direction Es'trixia was coming from and threw a forceful ball of energy; this time the energy fizzled in midstream.

"It will be weak, Louie," Onyx shouted over the wind, "the eclipse will affect everything even Es'trixia's magic."

Juggle thought quickly pulling out the amethyst found in Cave Saphical from his satchel. He threw it in Es'trixia's path. As the amethyst hit her she was thrown back in the air, giving the escapees extra time to gain pace.

Summer could see the palace in the near distance and prayed her father was ready with an army.

When the unicorns landed and before they'd even stopped, all passengers had jumped off and ran towards the palace gates.

Summer could only think of one person at the moment that could help their situation, her father.

"Father!" she shouted at the top of her voice.

Mardy appeared on the balcony above the courtyard. He looked down and saw his daughter and her friends running towards the palace. Mardy then looked in the distance and saw Es'trixia in the air followed by Julique.

An alarm sounded immediately.

The moon was close to covering the sun.

Onyx needed to keep the scroll in her possession until the eclipse had passed.

Mardy flew down to the gates followed by an army of angels behind him. He waved his hands out to his side and a thin vale of white diamonds showered the boundaries of the palace like a curtain.

Estrixa threw a wall of energy at them, pushing some of the vale out the way, but it wasn't enough. The Verlum army flew through the vale and towards Es'trixia. She managed to dodge them and slip in through the hole in the vale she had made, and into the same courtyard Onyx now stood.

Mardy turned and flew, with force, towards her.

A battle between good and evil ensued. It was like a light show, until Es'trixia pulled out the staff of the gods that was once Louie's. Mardy froze knowing that, with his power and hers combined, the staff could easily become confused and think of them both as its enemy.

Julique finally arrived but stood in the background knowing he needed to bide his moment to grab the scroll.

It was going to be too late. The moon was practically covering the sun. Julique knew if he was going to give it one last attempt it had to be now. He pounced onto Onyx throwing her to the ground and landing on top of her. The scroll flew through the air and landed away from Onyx's reach. She tried to scramble to her knees and reach for the scroll but Julique pinned her down. Onyx struggled against his grip trying to fight him off but he had taken her by surprise and now had the scroll within his reach. With one last lunge Julique grabbed the scroll.

"No!" Onyx screamed.

With no thought at all Louie pounced onto Juique's back. Julique let out a screech of pain but Louie didn't let go. He grabbed the top of his wing and ripped it downwards. Julique shrieked again and this time didn't stop. His hand dropped the scroll allowing Onyx to kick him off her and roll towards it.

Onyx scrambled her way closer.

In the same breath Es'trixia was now aware of the moon covering the sun. She knew it was too late unless she could get through the army of angels that were now pinning Julique down on the floor close to Onyx. With one last chance Es'trixia flew at extreme speed to where Onyx was now trying to grasp the scroll with her fingertips. Es'trixia was an arm's length away from clawing the scroll from Onyx when she was hit by an energy field that now surrounded Onyx. Es'trixia was thrown backwards in a spin of such force she continued spinning out of control, hitting the veil of diamonds. The diamonds embedded in her skin as she passed through them causing her to experience the most extreme pain she had ever felt. Mardy charged after her and watched the white flames that now encased her body diffuse. Es'trixia hung in the air disgruntled and defeated. She was furious.

Mardy watched the witch cloak herself in a green haze. Then she vanished.

The moon moved from in front of the sun quicker than it had taken to cover it, letting light out gradually.

Juggle ran over to Louie who still had a grip on Julique's wing. He hadn't noticed he was still on his back; he'd been so engrossed with watching the moon.

He quickly let go when Juggle came over to help.

Mardy walked to where Julique was now laying with guards surrounding him and stood looking down.

"You are despicable," Mardy snarled, still holding a graceful posture. "Guardians take him to the bridge."

"No please. No. Nooooo…" Julique struggled, with what energy he had left when the guardians dragged him off to the bridge that joined Tarania and Verlum.

The friends stood and watched as a shooting star landed in the distance. Louie knew this was Tyke and looked on knowing Julique was going to Limbo.

# Relief

Aster arrived not long after Tyke said his goodbyes to everyone, congratulating them all as he flew off.

Mardy invited everyone into the palace for a celebratory gathering.

The friends' first port of call was the infirmary. They all had injuries that needed to be fixed. It was the busiest the infirmary had been in a long time and very noisy too. The friends inspected one another's wounds judging who had the worst. They enjoyed being waited on by the pixies that were especially caring and professional and could have stayed in there all day. One by one they were mended and discharged, Louie being the first.

Louie sat alone in Mardy's untidy room. He was tired and ached all over although trying to digest everything that had happened, his mind spun with thoughts.

Onyx entered. "Do you mind if I join you, Louie? It's nice and quiet in here."

"No not at all." Louie tried to sit up to be polite but his body had different ideas, so he stayed slouched.

"I am so proud of you, Louie. You are a very brave young god." Onyx sat down at the table opposite Louie.

"I'm just glad we all survived. I still can't believe we managed to stop Es'trixia and Julique."

"Well you are half right. We have stopped Julique for now but we are nowhere near stopping Es'trixia."

Louie took a moment to realise what Onyx had just said. "What do you mean 'WE' are nowhere near stopping Es'trixia?"

"You know exactly what I mean, Louie. As long as Es'trixia is out there our worlds are in danger. She needs to be stopped. You and your friends are far from finishing your adventure. You have yet to finish what you started. She will not give up on planning her revenge until you, me and your friends have suffered or even worse, died."

Louie couldn't believe what he was hearing. No way could he go through any of that again; he was far from strong enough mentally or physically.

"I know at the moment, right now, it is the last thing you want to be thinking about, but you will have to soon and I will be there to guide you. We will work together."

Louie didn't like what he was hearing at all and felt too tired to think any more about it.

The words drifted away as Summer, Squidge, Juggle, Petra and Tia entered the room. Louie felt himself smile as he watched his friends fool around as usual.

Onyx quietly left the room allowing Louie to enjoy the victory with his friends.

She knew what lay ahead for all of them and most of all the power she would see them share eventually.

Turning back she took one more glance at Louie and whispered under her breath, "Goodbye, brave nephew." Louie looked towards the doorway and saw a shimmer of light. Onyx was gone.

# Fury

Es'trixia had returned to the only place she could hide, the underworld, although she would now have to find somewhere to stay. Julique's lair was useless just like he had been. The elders would know the whereabouts of his lair by now which meant her spells and potions would be destroyed.

Es'trixia hovered above the water in the middle of a black lake. She let out the loudest scream heard by all unfortunate enough to be down there.

'How could this happen? No one is more powerful,' she thought.

Her mind raced but her decision had been made; they were not going to get away with thinking they had beaten her. With one wave of her hand Es'trixia made the water separate beneath her feet allowing her to disappear within it.

As she lowered herself down one thought was for sure.

Revenge would be sweet and unexpected, especially to the young god and his friends. A nasty smile appeared on her face as she realised the pleasure she would have killing them all.